Will   Irma   Taranee   Cornelia   Hay Lin

# Finding Meridian

Adapted by ELIZABETH LENHARD

HarperCollins *Children's Books*

bi-bip bi-bip bi-bip bi-bip bi-bip

bi-bip
bi-bip

UMPH . . . STUPID ALARM CLOCK . . .

I'M NOT EVEN UP YET, AND ALREADY I'M TIRED!

"LOOK HOW PALE YOU ARE THIS MORNING. . . ."

I GUESS MUM'S RIGHT. . . . I'D BETTER GO TO BED EARLIER! I CAN JUST IMAGINE WHAT SHE'LL SAY. . . .

"WILL, LOOK AT YOUR FACE IN THE MIRROR. . . .

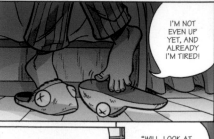

# ONE

I wonder if I'll *ever* get used to this? Will thought.

She felt the familiar quickening of her heart-beat. *Thump-thump-thumpity-thump.*

Then her mouth got dry. Her palms got wet. And finally, Will's vision went blurry. But when she blinked the haze away, she found that she was still witnessing the same incredible scene. Her friend, Hay Lin, had just snapped a huge cement pillar in two. The chunk of rock must have weighed five hundred pounds!

How had skinny little Hay Lin done it?

Simple – magic.

Yup, Will thought. She gazed at all four of her friends, scattered around the abandoned construction site. We're all magic – every one

of us. I still can't quite wrap my brain around it.

Judging from her friends' expressions, they were a bit weirded-out as well. Taranee was gripping her pink satchel with clenched fists. It was white knuckles, trembling fingers time, all the way.

Irma was Taranee's complete opposite. She was giggling so hard that her shaggy, honey-coloured pigtails were practically dancing.

Hay Lin's almond-shaped eyes were twinkling with a mixture of mischief and sheer determination.

And Cornelia was sticking out her bottom lip – she was all skepticism and sulkiness.

That about sums it up, Will thought, as she took in her friends' wild range of emotions. These magical powers are both fabulous and awful, thrilling and scary. They're dividing us, but they're also bringing us together.

Magic was what Will and her friends were all about these days. When they'd planned to hang out today, for instance, it hadn't been to lounge around a coffeehouse, chowing down on scones and gossiping about the cutest boys at their school, the Sheffield Institute.

No, instead, they were hiding behind this

construction site's tall, wooden fence, practising their magic.

It was clear that Hay Lin, at least, was getting pretty good at it! Not only had she just cracked that chunk of cement off its base as if she were plucking a leaf from a tree, she'd also whipped the huge, craggy block into the sky on a mystical swirl of air. Finally, she'd plunked the block down onto a slab of stone with a tremendous *crunch*.

Then Cornelia had stepped in. She'd stared at the block, her arms outstretched and her blue eyes steely.

With waves of power that were almost palpable, Cornelia had cracked the stone slab on which the cement block rested. It splintered like a thin sheet of ice. Ropy vines poked through the cracks like mischievous green snakes. In the blink of an eye, they coiled their way completely around the block.

Then Cornelia's eyes got even squintier. Her mouth twisted into a stiff smile. She concentrated so hard her long, silky, blonde hair stood on end. And then – *skrump*! The ropy vines squeezed the cement block into smithereens! Shards of rock flew in every direction.

Taranee jumped, her round spectacles going askew on her nose. Hay Lin scowled. Cornelia had totally one-upped her. And Irma, who was always clashing with Cornelia, simply rolled her eyes and pretended to be bored.

Meanwhile, Cornelia just folded her slender arms across her chest and smirked.

"I bet you can't do that," she said to her friends.

Will shuddered at the memory.

The crazy thing, she thought, is that we can *all* do that. Or something like it.

Will looked around at her new friends. She'd only known them for a little while. She'd met them on her first day at the Sheffield Institute, right after she and her Mum had moved to this breezy seaside city called Heatherfield. The girls' friendship had started normally enough. They'd gabbed about crushes, complained about history homework, and commiserated about pain-in-the-butt siblings. But it hadn't been long before the five girls had discovered that they were anything but normal.

Cornelia could control the earth (as was obvious from the shattered cement block). Hay Lin – who was so tiny she looked as if the wind could carry her away – had the powers of air. Wishy-washy Irma was all about water. And Taranee could hold fire in the palm of her hand.

And me, Will thought with a shrug, well, that's the craziest part. I somehow ended up as the leader of our whole crew – Will, Irma, Taranee, Cornelia, Hay Lin. Otherwise known as W.i.t.c.h.

She glanced with irritation at the heavens. That's where she imagined the mystical beings who'd given them their powers resided.

Nice work, Will thought. I can't believe you made me – awkward, frog-collecting Will Vandom – the leader of these girls.

But before Will could get too deep into an angstfest, Irma interrupted her thoughts. She was offering her opinion on Cornelia's feat of shattering the pillar.

"Oh, that's just *amazing*, Cornelia," she said sarcastically. "Actually, I've never seen anything so silly in my entire life."

Cornelia sniffed and turned her back on Irma.

Then Irma sniffed and turned her back on Cornelia.

And then Taranee looked expectantly at Will.

Uh, right, Will thought. I guess it's leadership time!

She stepped forward and eyed Irma and Cornelia nervously.

"Oh, come on," she said with a nervous laugh. "Would you two stop bickering? We're here to practise, not fight!"

"Will's right," Taranee agreed. "We should help each other. We're a team now. . . ."

"I guess you're right, Taranee," Hay Lin piped up. She was now sitting pensively on top of another cement block nearby. "But we don't know how our powers work yet! If only Grandma had told us something more before she . . . passed away."

Hay Lin's reedy, mournful voice trailed off. Will cringed for her friend. Yan Lin's death was still fresh for them all. And what was worse, Hay Lin's tiny, mysterious grandmother had died before the girls could ask her everything they yearned to know about their magical new powers.

Yan Lin would have been able to explain everything, Will thought. After all, she was magical once, too. She was the one who informed us of our magical destiny.

Will was still trying to grasp the things that Yan Lin had told them over tea and cookies in Hay Lin's cosy kitchen.

For starters, Yan Lin told them about worlds that existed somewhere in the universe, far away from earth.

In Candracar – which was a sort of other-worldly temple – benevolent, mystical beings kept watch over all things good and just.

Then there was the land of Metamoor. Evil creatures from Metamoor wanted to take over the world. And only one thing was stopping them – the Veil. The Veil was a supernatural barrier, placed around the earth to keep bad things out.

There was just one catch, Yan Lin had told the girls. The dawn of the millennium had weakened the Veil. Twelve portals had opened in its invisible fabric. And now, terrifying, evil creatures from Metamoor were beginning to break through those portals into Heatherfield.

One of the girls' friends, Elyon, had even gone through the portal. Elyon had been miss-ing for a while now. Just before she'd disappeared, she'd asked Will, Hay Lin, and Irma to accompany her on a date at the school gym. But when the three girls had arrived, Elyon had been nowhere to be seen. There *were* however, a couple of murderous creatures waiting for the girls. And they'd almost managed to toss the girls into a bottomless chasm!

Later, Elyon – or some evil ghost of Elyon – had drawn all five girls into the basement of her abandoned house. There she'd tried to pull Hay Lin into a portal that had opened up in the basement wall.

Both times, the girls had been transformed into Guardians of the Veil. It had started with the Heart of Candracar – a shimmering, magical orb that Yan Lin had given to Will. The orb lay inside Will's body. Usually, it was dormant. But if Will and her friends needed it for any reason, Will could call the Heart. Then it would appear in her palm. Its power transformed the girls into their magical selves – young women with long legs, mature faces and bodies, and fabulous outfits.

And, best of all, Will thought with a giggle, we have magical powers and strength enough to kick any bad guy's butt!

Still, the girls had far from mastered their magic. Will didn't know how much power they were capable of.

She also didn't know how much they'd need. The girls had fought off a hulking, blue lug of a creature and a vengeful, dark-voiced snake man in the gym. In Elyon's basement, they had conquered brick walls that had come to life and tried to bury them alive.

But Will had a feeling that she and her friends hadn't yet seen the worst of Metamoor's evil soldiers.

And *that's* why they were at this construction site, training for battle.

And arguing.

Will turned to Hay Lin. Her face – usually so sunny – was clouded with grief for her grandmother.

"We'll have to do this without her," Will said to Hay Lin softly. "That's all."

"Do you really think that's enough?" Cornelia broke in. She kicked a cement shard across the grass.

"I mean," she continued angrily, "look around you! We can do magic! We can transfigure things! We can command water, air, earth, and fire. But we don't know why!"

"Well," Hay Lin said wanly, "we're the Guardians of the Veil."

"I know that," Cornelia snapped. "But why? Why us?!"

Irma's scowl turned into a flirty smile. She cocked one round hip and wiggled her eyebrows.

"Because we're so pretty," she cooed. "Don't you think?"

"I'm not joking, Irma," Cornelia said with a glower. Then she turned her back on Irma, Hay Lin, and Taranee and glared straight at Will. "Our lives have changed, Will. But we didn't choose it."

"You're right," Will responded with a shrug. "But I don't know. I'm as confused as you are."

Cornelia's hands scrunched up into frustrated fists.

"I thought our *leader* always had the right answer," she said. Her voice was full of sullen bitterness. Full of challenge.

Will's temper flared. Normally, she was a bit deferential to Cornelia. After all – Cornelia was the *true* leader in the group. She was tall and willowy and effortlessly popular. She had megaconfidence and she was usually pretty nice, to boot.

But now she was being unfair. And Will wasn't going to let her get away with it.

"Well, you know what, Cornelia? I *don't* have the answers," she blurted out. "As a matter of fact, I'm not even sure I'm meant to be your leader. As you said, Cornelia, we didn't choose this!"

Hay Lin huffed in frustration and grabbed her pink-and-purple backpack. She'd stashed it next to the cement block she was using as a stool.

Unzipping the pack, she pulled out a weighty, dusty, blue book. They'd found the book in Elyon's basement, right after they had chased Elyon and her Metamoorian thug back through the portal.

"I'm sure the solution to all our problems is in this book," Hay Lin said. She held it in her lap and gazed at her friends hopefully.

"You're wrong, Hay Lin," Cornelia said with a sneer. "This book is just another of the problems."

Taranee gave Cornelia a furtive glance and then joined Hay Lin in examining the book.

The edges of its pages were scuffed and ragged. But its spine? That was unbroken.

"Did you manage to get it open?" Taranee asked Hay Lin.

"Not yet," Hay Lin sighed. "And I tried everything!" To demonstrate, she grabbed the front and back covers of the book and yanked at them with all her strength. But the book remained firmly closed.

As Hay Lin struggled with the book, Will felt the back of her neck prickle in a familiar way. Then a wave of dizziness washed over her. She could almost feel her freckled cheeks go pale. And when she lifted a hand to her forehead, her fingers were trembling.

"There's . . . there's a spell on that book," Will gasped, staggering away from Hay Lin. "Put it away!"

## TWO

Irma ran over to Will. The sight of her friend all pale and shaky made her feel a little fluttery herself.

"Do you have that strange sensation again?" Irma cried.

Will nodded fuzzily. Out of the corner of her eye, Irma saw Hay Lin scurry to zip the mysterious blue book back into her backpack. Instantly, Will's shakes began to lessen. She blinked slowly. Then she raised her head and looked Irma in the eyes.

Irma tried to flash Will a reassuring grin, but inside her gut was an uneasy rumbling. Sort of like the feeling she got after eating one too many bowls of Fizzing Frosted Corn Pops.

This isn't the first time Will's had an attack like this, Irma mused nervously. Will had also gone limp and trembly at the Halloween party, right before all sorts of sci-fi craziness had broken loose. And it had happened again after Yan Lin's funeral, when Hay Lin had first seen the ghostly Elyon.

And now, Irma thought, our leader's been hit again – by that annoying old book.

"Ugh," Will sighed. "It's really strange. I feel dizzy. . . . I have butterflies in my stomach. . . ."

Then she tried to smile.

"I guess I'll get used to it in the end," she offered.

Irma sighed with relief. She really wanted Will to be okay – for Will's sake, but also for her own peace of mind.

I mean, Irma thought, if the keeper of the Heart of Candracar loses it, what'll happen to the rest of us?!

Irma could never say anything like that out loud. Talk about dragging down a party. So instead, she responded in her usual fashion – with a quip.

"Maybe," she said to Will, "this dizzy spell

is all about something you had for breakfast!"

"I don't think so," Will laughed. "It doesn't last long. . . . And it's so difficult to describe. I mean . . . I feel the same way every time our maths teacher calls me up to the blackboard!"

"Ah!" Hay Lin said with a glint in her eyes. "That just means you're scared."

"Wait a minute!" Irma said, her eyes getting wide again. "Maybe Will gets that particular feeling for a reason. Do you think our maths teacher could be a creature from Metamoor?"

"Mrs. Rudolph?" Taranee said with a gulp. "But she's such a nice old lady!"

Irma walked over to Taranee and slung an arm over her shoulders.

"Things aren't always what they seem, Taranee," she said. "Devoting your entire life to maths is simply *not* human."

Taranee guffawed, and Irma smiled with satisfaction. It took a lot of talent to make Taranee laugh these days. But when Irma glanced from Taranee to Will, her smirk faded. Will was wiping a sheen of cold sweat off her upper lip and looking seriously freaked out. Irma's stomach swooped back to its nervous fluttering.

Wouldn't it be cool, she thought wistfully, if our maths teacher *were* our biggest enemy? I would *so* prefer a pop quiz to another fight with Metamoorian ghouls. Irma pictured the giant blue monster who'd almost tossed her into a pit that first night at the gym. She shuddered. But before she could imagine herself in a full-blown horrorfest, Will recovered and got back on track.

"All right, then," she said, trying to sound bright and cheerful. "The break's over. Shall we start?"

"Sure!" Hay Lin said. She pulled her knee up beneath her pointy chin. "I'd like to experiment with a little combined action. C'mon, let's try! I wonder what happens if we combine . . . let's see . . . the powers of water and earth."

"Maybe you'll get the power of . . . mud?" Irma giggled. She glanced around at her friends, expecting a laugh in return. Everyone gave her one – except, of course, Cornelia. *She* merely glared.

Irma sucked in her breath quickly.

Could Cornelia *be* any more annoying? she wondered. When she's not being all magicker-than-thou, she's supersour!

Not that Irma wasn't used to Cornelia's well-crafted pout. They'd always been at odds with each other.

Face it, Irma told herself. If we were music, I'd be grunge and Cornelia would be techno. I'm a softie, and Cornelia's Miss Right Angle. We are brunette and blonde, night and day.

And that had always worked fine when they were just two normal girls. But now they were Guardians of the Veil – fighting off evil and saving the world together!

Ugh! Irma thought. If only I could save the world with Will, Taranee, Hay Lin, and a couple of cute boys! She shot a glare of her own at Cornelia. Then she rubbed her hands together. She'd show her! It was time for a little magic.

But of course, the oh-so-on-top-of-it-all Cornelia had been thinking the same thing.

"I'll go first!" she said.

"No," Irma retorted, "*I'll* go first."

She whirled around to face the empty stretch of grass behind the construction site. She raised her hands out in front of her. Almost immediately, she felt her magic begin to bubble up within her. She wasn't even sure what she intended to do. But she knew it would be spectacular. And it would definitely be wet!

Irma's vision went blurry, the way it did when she opened her eyes under water. She felt weightless – no, buoyant. And her outstretched hands began to take on a bluish cast. Irma's fingers were trembling. Her pigtails trembled. Even the frayed threads dangling from the hem of her denim skirt shook!

Finally, she gasped, as a cool rush of power surged through her. At the same time, a swirly, blue swoosh of magic flew out of her hands! It looped the loop through the air toward the center of the lawn.

Irma watched in awe as the magic – *her* magic – danced through the air.

Of course, her moment of singular glory didn't last long. When Irma glanced Cornelia's way, her arms were thrust out before her, too. Cornelia's long hair began to dance and flutter behind her back. Her blue eyes darkened to a mossy green. And then, a whoosh of emerald-coloured magic rushed out of *her* palms. It arced neatly over Irma's squiggly, blue stream.

*Fwooooom!*

Both magical rays landed on the same spot. Irma gulped, and all five girls froze, waiting to see what would happen next.

They didn't have to wait long.

The earth beneath their feet begin to quake. And rumble. It practically growled!

And then – it erupted.

*FWOOOOOOOOSSHHH!* A massive geyser of water shot straight out of the earth, bubbling high into the air! Irma and Cornelia, who were standing only a few feet away from the instant Old Faithful, were knocked off their feet.

*"Aaagh!"* they shrieked. The plume sent bits of dirt, grass, and rock flying all around them. Then the geyser reached its peak – and fell. Torrents of water began to rain down upon the girls.

Irma cringed as the cold water hit her. But her discomfort didn't last more than an instant. After all, water was Irma's best friend. Even when she was wearing one of her favourite out-fits, she never really minded a downpour.

And here's the other thing, Irma thought gleefully. We're being spattered with drops of water. *Not* clods of dirt. Water has totally trumped earth! I've won! My magic has kicked Cornelia's magic's butt. And don't think she doesn't know it!

Cornelia was scowling down at her own

soaked sweater and sopping hair. Then she turned on Irma in a rage.

"See what you did!" she yelled.

"Poor girl," Irma taunted. "You're gonna need a barrel of hair conditioner to fix that mop!"

Irma laughed and put her wet hands on her wet hips. Then she got ready for Cornelia to hurl a zinger back at her. Irma knew the drill. This was the part where Cornelia said something snide.

Then Irma would respond with something snotty.

Cornelia would make a retort. And then Irma . . . it was the law of the universe, or at least, of Sheffield Institute.

Night and day, Irma thought again.

But when she glanced through the sudden, magical rain shower at her pals, her grin faded. Hay Lin and Taranee were bewildered. And Will was looking seriously stressed. Will looked from Cornelia to Irma to the geyser. She chewed on her lip. She crossed her arms over her skinny stomach. Her shoulders hunched up so high they almost touched her ears!

Somehow, Irma knew just what Will was

thinking. She was thinking of Metamoor.

And monsters.

And huge, nasty portals ready to gobble them all up.

And then she was thinking about Saturday morning TV stuff – like cooperation and compassion and hard work. She was thinking that if the Guardians didn't work together, they were going to fail. The world would be doomed.

How did Irma know Will was thinking about all these things? She knew because she was sort of thinking along the same lines.

But it was Will who decided to *do* something about it. Suddenly, she flung her arms out in front of her. They pulsated with the Heart of Candracar's pink-tinted magic. And then Will screamed, "*Stop!*"

*Blub, blub, blub, blub . . .*

Irma gasped and returned her gaze to her giant plume of water. It had obeyed Will's order and completely petered out. In just a few seconds, it had drained itself to a mere trickle. Then the last whiffs of her and Cornelia's magic evaporated with a fizzle.

Irma, along with the other Guardians, turned back to gaze at Will. In the aftermath of her big power surge, Will was looking more shy and sheepish than ever. She glanced at her four friends and giggled self-consciously. She shuffled one sneaker through the damp grass. And then she shrugged and smoothed back her dripping hair.

Oh, brother, Irma thought wearily. Cornelia and I are at war. Taranee's a total scaredy-cat. Hay Lin's mega-sad. And Will's totally embarrassed about being the leader. And *we're* gonna save the world? This I've gotta see!

# THREE

It was Monday morning. Maths class. Twenty-four entire hours since Irma's magic had completely trounced Cornelia's at the abandoned construction site.

But Cornelia was still seething. In fact, she was clenching her pencil so hard, it started to splinter in her hand. *That* made Cornelia catch her breath.

I've got to chill! she thought. What am I so stressed about? I am *so* going to get this magic thing down. I just have to look at it as a challenge. Like the jumps I've been trying to land at skating practise. Next time Irma and I face off, I'm totally going to win. I can feel it.

The thought brought a stiff little smile to Cornelia's face. But it didn't succeed in making her shoulders relax or her jaw unclench.

Face it, Cornelia thought with a sigh. Winning a magic contest isn't going to make me happy. What would make me happy is withdrawing from this battle altogether! Did I ask for these powers? No! Do I want them? Not much.

But even as those thoughts darted around her head – the way they did about once an hour those days – Cornelia knew they weren't *completely* true.

The fact was, the idea of having magical powers that nobody else had (well, except for her fellow Guardians) made Cornelia shiver with delight.

So, what was the damage, really?

It was the fact that she couldn't control her new power. She *hated* being a newbie at anything! That was why she studied so hard and spent so many hours at the ice rink. If Cornelia was going to do anything, she wanted to do it well.

She even cared about excelling in maths, a feat that was especially hard to pull off today. On Mondays, Cornelia's maths class was two whole hours long. And not just any two hours. They were the last – and the sleepiest – two hours of the school day.

Mrs. Rudolph was sitting at the front of the classroom, droning on about binomials. Cornelia was dutifully taking notes. In between jottings, she glanced around the classroom. Her gaze froze on Will, who was sitting a few desks ahead of Cornelia. Even from her seat behind Will's, Cornelia could tell that her friend was conked out. Her chin was resting on top of her hands and her back was lifting in deep, regular breaths.

Apparently, Cornelia wasn't the only one who'd noticed.

"Will!" Mrs. Rudolph said suddenly. She folded her hands smugly on top on her desk. "Would you like to join in on the subject we were discussing?"

Will lifted her head woozily.

"Huh . . . ?" she muttered.

Uh-oh, Cornelia thought. A fellow witch is in trouble. In fact, she's in danger of completely humiliating herself!

Will jumped out of her chair and stood at attention in the aisle. She looked around and blinked blearily. Then she turned back to Mrs. Rudolph, whose plump face looked quite amused behind her big, tinted glasses.

"Sorry, ma'am," Will squeaked in a shaky voice. "I didn't get what you asked. I . . . I wasn't listening."

"That's why I asked you," Mrs. Rudolph said. She stood up and stepped out from behind her desk. She folded her hands behind her wide back and gazed at Will with a mixture of sternness and amusement. "You must know your lesson really well, since you can afford not to listen. We were reviewing Ruffini's theorem. Would you like to complete my explanation?"

Mrs. Rudolph tossed Will a piece of chalk. Will caught it with a gulp. A flush of scarlet surged to her cheeks.

"Uh . . . well . . . of course," Will stammered. "The theorem of . . . what's his name?"

Mrs. Rudolph sank back into her desk chair and gave Will a dry look.

"Ruffini, Will," she said in her deep, throaty voice. "Maths, you know . . . binomials . . . polynomials . . . $x$ squared . . ."

"Oh sure, I got it," Will said with a nervous giggle. Her shoulders hunched up to her ears, the way they always did when she wanted to sink into the floor. She shuffled up to the blackboard and held her chalk an inch away from the blackboard. Her other hand fluttered up to her chin. She glanced at the ceiling, as if she hoped the correct answer might drop through it and smack her on the head. She muttered, "Well . . . Ruffini's theorem . . . let me see. . . . hmm– . . ."

Cornelia knew Will was panicking. Cornelia was also bored stiff with the cruel game that Mrs. Rudolph was playing.

"Take your time," the maths teacher was saying to Will. "We're in no hurry. We have a good fifteen minutes before the end of the class."

That's when Cornelia knew what she was going to do. All it took was a flick of her right index finger. A swirl of barely-there, celery-green magic flowed out of her fingertip. Cornelia narrowed her eyes, focusing on the magical wisp. She watched it float up toward the ceiling, then bobble its way toward the classroom door.

She smirked as the magic curled like a woolly scarf around the bell that hung just over the doorway.

Fifteen minutes can be a long, long time, my friend, Cornelia thought, glancing at the still-paralysed Will. But you know what they say – time flies when you're having fun!

*Brrrrrinnnng!* The bell began to ring loudly. Cornelia's smile grew a bit wider and she nodded with satisfaction as her filament of green magic melted into the air.

Will's eyes widened in confusion.

Mrs. Rudolph's mouth popped open in surprise.

The rest of the kids in the class didn't seem to care that the bell was early. They were too busy shaking the sleepy fog from their heads and jumping giddily out of their chairs. They bounded towards the door, waving to Mrs. Rudolph in elation.

"See you, Mrs. Rudolph!" they called, pulling on their backpacks and rushing from the classroom.

"But . . . wait a minute!" the flummoxed teacher cried. "Where are you going?"

As Cornelia grabbed her messenger bag, she heard Mrs. Rudolph mutter, "I can't believe that! The bell rang earlier than usual today."

Cornelia waited by the door as Will hurried back to her desk to stuff her notebook and maths textbook into her pink backpack.

"Saved by the bell, huh?" Cornelia whispered.

"Thanks," Will breathed back.

"You owe me one!"

Cornelia grinned and began to flounce out of the classroom. Will was right on her heels.

"All right, then," Will called out to Mrs. Rudolph happily. "Good-bye, ma'am!"

"Wait a minute, Will," Mrs. Rudolph called out to her. Cornelia gulped and stopped to hover just outside the classroom door. Did Mrs. Rudolph think Will was responsible for the early bell? Was she going to get in trouble?

Cornelia cocked her head anxiously and eavesdropped on the sudden student-teacher confab.

"You hadn't done your homework, had you?" Mrs. Rudolph asked Will.

"It's . . . it's just that theorem," Will protested. "I tried – not much, that's true. But I did try! I really don't understand it!"

Mrs. Rudolph led Will out into the hall. Cornelia tailed them as they walked towards the school's front door.

"How are you getting along in Heatherfield, Will?" Mrs. Rudolph asked. "I mean . . . you've been here for a little while. Everything all right?"

Cornelia raised her eyebrows. Who knew maths teachers had an ounce of sympathy in them? she thought. Or maybe even two.

"Everything's fine," Will said, flashing a grateful grin at the teacher. "Why do you ask?"

"I know maths isn't much fun," Mrs. Rudolph said, patting Will on the shoulder. "But I've noticed . . . you always look so pensive and absentminded."

"Things aren't so easy for me right now," Will admitted.

You can say *that* again, Cornelia thought.

"But I'm fine," Will assured Mrs. Rudolph.

"I'm glad to hear that," the teacher replied. They'd reached the sidewalk in front of the school. Mrs. Rudolph paused and faced Will. "By the way, I could help you with that theorem if you like. I don't usually do private tutoring, but I'll make an exception for you. If that can help you be more attentive during my class, that is. . . ."

"I– " Will stammered. "Thank you so much, Mrs. Rudolph!"

"Any afternoon would do," the maths teacher said kindly. "What do you think? I'm sure an hour or so will be enough."

"Great," Will said. "You choose the day."

"Why don't I call you to let you know?" Mrs. Rudolph proposed. While Will wrote her cell phone number down for the teacher, Taranee walked up to Cornelia's side. She raised her eyebrows as Mrs. Rudolph slipped Will's number into her purse and walked away. Then Will joined Taranee and Cornelia.

"Will!" Taranee giggled. "Since when have you been *friends* with our maths teacher?!"

"She was so nice to me," Will said with a befuddled look on her face. "I totally expected to get an F!"

"And you certainly would have gotten one," Cornelia smirked, "if *someone* hadn't saved you."

As Will flashed Cornelia another grateful smile, Cornelia felt a sense of peace wash over her. Maybe she *was* finally getting a handle on her magic. It was about time! She breathed in a big gulp of crisp autumn air and glanced across the street. Maybe she'd actually enjoy the afternoon now. She could start with a smoothie from the restaurant on the corner. Lots of people from Heatherfield hung out there. It was the best place to hang out after school or work.

Cornelia peered over towards the sidewalk café to see if there were a table available in the sun.

Darn, she thought. Looks as if every seat's taken. I wonder if anyone is about to lea–

"Oh!" Cornelia blurted out.

She blinked and shook her head. Was she seeing what she thought she was seeing?

"What?" Will said, looking at Cornelia quizzically.

"Uh, it looks like making friends with the Sheffield teachers must be a family hobby," Cornelia said. "That looks just like your mother, having a 'meeting' with our history teacher!"

She tried to sound breezy. But as she watched Will's face go white, she felt a little pang of sadness for her. It had to be awful for Will. Not only were her parents divorced, but now Will's mum was hanging out with Mr. Collins. Yuck!

Taranee sent Will a sympathetic look, too, but Will didn't notice. She stood frozen on the curb, staring across the street.

The scene did not look good.

Not only were Ms. Vandom and Mr. Collins

making eyes at each other over their meal, they were also *sharing*! As Mr. Collins handed a fork to Ms. Vandom, Cornelia was sure she saw his hand linger on top of hers.

Cornelia glanced at Will. She must have seen that, too. She was holding her breath, and tears had already begun sparkling in her eyes. And when Ms. Vandom gave Mr. Collins's hand a squeeze, Will gasped out loud. Then she spun around and began running down the sidewalk, her loafers pounding the cement angrily.

Cornelia saw Ms. Vandom's head turn towards the sound. Will's mother jumped out of her seat in alarm.

"Will!" she cried, rushing out of the café. Ms. Vandom crossed the street to chase after her daughter.

"Go away," Will shouted at her mum over her shoulder. "Leave me alone!"

But Ms. Vandom didn't listen. She caught up to Will and grabbed her hand.

"Will!" she gasped. "What's the matter with you?"

"I . . . I saw you sitting out there with him," Will spat. "You embarrassed me in front of my friends!"

That made Cornelia give Taranee a guilty glance. Taranee motioned in the opposite direction. Let's get out of here, her expression said.

Good idea, Cornelia thought. It's time to get out of earshot before things get more mortifying for all of us.

As she and Taranee tiptoed away from the scene, Cornelia couldn't help but overhear the end of the fight.

"What do you mean?" Ms. Vandom was saying to Will. "Dean's just a friend."

"Dean!" Will shrieked. "You're already calling him by his first name?"

"It's you who are embarrassing me, now," Ms. Vandom said in exasperation. "This was just a business meeting. Your school and Simultech are– "

"Oh, come on!" Will accused. "You were holding his hand. I saw you!"

With that, Will burst into tears. She turned to run away again. That time, Ms. Vandom let her go. When Cornelia peeked back at Will's mother, her face was anguished.

Mr. Collins stole up behind her and put his hands on her shoulders.

"Susan," he said apologetically.

"Oh, Dean," Ms. Vandom sighed. "What'll I do?"

Whoa, Cornelia thought as she finally slunk around the corner, trailing Taranee by several feet. Talk about a trauma.

She grimaced in sympathy for Will. She couldn't imagine what it must be like to have a broken family. To see your mother holding hands with a stranger.

And on top of that, to have to be the keeper of the Heart of Candracar.

Something in Cornelia's chest tightened, just a bit.

*Hmmm*, she thought grimly. I guess we'll just have to wait and see if Will can handle drama on the home front *and* lead W.i.t.c.h at the same time!

# FOUR

Will took the steps to her loft two at a time, her heart pounding. If she didn't get behind a closed door immediately, she would die!

Okay, she *might not* die. But she would definitely humiliate herself – by blubbering in public. And she'd already had all the mortification she could possibly stand today.

Finally, Will reached her floor in the old building where she and her mum lived. Will could hear her feet hitting the cement floor with echoey thuds as she raced down the hall.

She gasped with relief as she made it to her door. She unlocked it and slumped inside.

Then, at last, she let go.

Flopping back against the door, she let her face crumple. Her tears finally spilled out of her eyes and streamed down her cheeks. Her breath came in big, sobbing gasps.

As she cried, the scene played itself over and over in her mind: she'd actually seen her mum making goo-goo eyes at her *history teacher*.

She'd seen their hands touch.

She'd seen her mum giggle like a little girl.

And then, Mum had denied the whole thing. She'd lied to her own daughter!

The thought launched Will into a fresh round of sobs. Stumbling into the kitchen, she grabbed a paper towel and blew her nose loudly. She wiped away the new flood of tears.

Finally, she was all cried out. Sniffling list-lessly, she slumped to the kitchen pantry. She pulled out a loaf of soft, fluffy, white bread and a jar of chocolate-hazelnut spread. She flopped down at the kitchen table with a plate, pulled out three slices of bread, and smeared them with the gooey chocolate spread.

"Bread and chocolate," she muttered. "The perfect food for despair."

But when she lifted one of the fragrant slices to her lips, she found she was too despondent even to take a bite. In disgust, she tossed the snack back onto her plate. Then she shoved the plate away and folded her arms on the table. She rested her chin on top of her folded hands and sighed.

She tried hard to remember what life had been like when she'd lived in Fadden Hills. Her parents had been happy together. She'd been a typical, oblivious kid racing from school to swim practise to sleepover parties without a care in the world.

Those days were *so* over.

"Are you okay, Miss Will?"

Will glanced at the refrigerator. The ice lever in the door was waggling and a clipped British voice was rumbling out of the water spout.

I rest my case, Will sighed. Appliances that talk? Definitely not normal.

Still, she couldn't help but smile. She had to admit, being able to communicate with her fridge, TV, and computer *did* make her apartment feel less lonely!

"I'm fine, James," she said quietly.

"Are you sure?" James the fridge continued. "Usually, when you open that jar, it means you're sad."

"Well," Will said with a sigh, "today I'd

need a whole barrel of chocolate to make me feel better."

Swirling her butter knife idly through the chocolate spread, she felt her eyes begin to tear up again.

If only I could have a normal family like my friends. A family where people just love each other, she thought.

Propping her head on her hand, she thought of Cornelia's picture-perfect family – a mother, a father, and two daughters, all living happily in a glamorous penthouse apartment. She pictured Cornelia and her little sister, Lilian, bopping each other with pillows and jumping on the bed. They laughed hysterically while their mum smiled at them from the bedroom doorway.

A family just like all the others . . . Will daydreamed. Without any secrets. Without any mysteries.

Cornelia and her giggly sister shimmered away and Will's mind filled with the image of Taranee hanging at home. Her shy friend was sitting on a couch, reading a book, while her big brother, Peter, loped through the living room, carrying his surfboard. Peter would be on his way to the beach, braving the cold to catch the last good waves of the day.

Will could almost feel the comfort Taranee got from her brash big brother. Where Taranee was shy, Peter was all confidence and kindness. Will knew Peter made Taranee feel safe. But who did she have to make her feel safe?

And what would it be like to have a family like Hay Lin's? Will wondered sadly.

She pictured Hay Lin's parents, sitting down to an early dinner before their Chinese restaurant started to fill up with hungry customers. In their warm, cluttered kitchen – a cosy, pistachio-green room directly upstairs from the Silver Dragon's dining room – Hay Lin's pretty mother would be cupping a bowl of steaming seafood soup in her palm. Her husband might be scooping up a mouthful of rice with his red chopsticks.

When Hay Lin got home, a warm dinner would be waiting for her. Along with the smiles of her two parents.

"Mmmmm," Will sighed wistfully. She slowly screwed the lid back onto her jar of chocolate and tossed the cold loaf of bread back into the pantry. "A family without any lies. Must be nice."

# FIVE

I can't believe my parents bought my lie, Hay Lin thought.

What's more, Hay Lin couldn't believe she'd *told* the lie. She'd just called home from the school pay phone. And she'd made sure to call at just the moment her mum would be putting dinner on the table. She had put on a breezy voice and told her mother, "I'm at the library with Irma. I'll be home later."

Hay Lin *was* with Irma – but they weren't at the library. In fact, they were loitering outside of Mrs. Rudolph's house, a few blocks away from school. Hay Lin cringed with guilt as she pictured her parents at home. Right now, they'd be starting their meal, with soup served in Hay Lin's favourite pink-and-white bowls.

Maybe it was her favourite soup, too – sizzling rice. The thought of the crunchy clusters of rice and the crispy vegetables in her grandmother's famous soup recipe made her mouth water.

Then she imagined her dad looking in confusion at her empty chair.

"Is Hay Lin not coming home for dinner?" her dad would ask as her mum placed a tray of warm food in front of him.

"She called five minutes ago," her mum would say. "She's in the library, doing homework with Irma."

"She always calls at the last minute," her dad would say with a scowl. "Hay Lin must learn – this is not a restaurant!"

"But dear," her mum would say with a placid little smile. "This *is* a restaurant."

Hay Lin couldn't help but giggle at that part. That was her mum. Straightforward and honest to a fault.

Not like Hay Lin.

She cringed again and pictured her dad's disapproving frown. She knew he wasn't as trusting as Mum. There was definitely going to be an interrogation when Hay Lin got home.

And who knew when *that* was happening?

*Rumble-rumble-rumble.* Irma looked at Hay Lin.

"What was that sound?" she asked with wide eyes.

"It was my stomach," Hay Lin whined. "I'm starving. It's late! Let's go home."

Irma shook her head stubbornly.

"I want to find out Mrs. Rudolph's secrets first," she insisted.

*That* was why she and Hay Lin had been camped out behind their maths teacher's, ever since school had let out.

Hay Lin rolled her eyes as she remembered how Irma had dragged her there. School had just let out. In fact, the bell had rung fifteen minutes early! Hay Lin was psyched. She'd skipped out of Sheffield and run into Irma at their usual meeting spot at the base of the west steps.

"School's out early!" Hay Lin had announced. "It's a sign!"

"A sign of what?" Irma had asked. She was only half-listening as she peered at something across the courtyard.

"A sign that we should go do something!"

Hay Lin had said, dancing in a little circle around her friend.

"We have fifteen extra minutes in our lives," she continued. "We can use them to make a quick trip to Baubles."

"Why do you want to go there?" Irma said, rolling her eyes. "There's an art-supply store right near your apartment."

"Yeah, but Baubles is the best," Hay Lin whined. "They have the most amazing oil paints – every colour you can imagine. And beads! Scads and scads of beads. Maybe we could go and grab some beads. I could make you a necklace."

That idea caught Irma's attention. She fingered the glittery choker that was already strung around her neck and looked at Hay Lin with a defiant pout.

"I don't know, Hay Lin," she said. "I have something else in mind. . . ."

With that, Irma began to drift across the courtyard. Hay Lin sighed. Irma was very stubborn. But she was also the most fun friend Hay Lin had. So she'd shrugged and followed Irma toward the sidewalk. The girls hid behind a pillar and watched the scene – Will was talking to

Mrs. Rudolph, and Cornelia and Taranee were standing nearby.

"*Oooh*," Hay Lin breathed in Irma's ear. "Scandal. Mrs. Rudolph is talking to Will about . . . *maths homework!*"

Irma had giggled. Then she'd stared at Mrs. Rudolph again.

"Why would Mrs. Rudolph take such an interest in Will?" she wondered out loud.

"Uh, I don't know," Hay Lin said sarcastically. "Because Will's in her algebra class, perhaps?"

"Or maybe because Mrs. Rudolph really *is* a creature from Metamoor," Irma said, rubbing her hands together. Hay Lin saw little sparks of watery blue magic shoot out from between Irma's palms.

"Hello?" Hay Lin said. "May I remind you what a creature from Metamoor looks like? We're talking eight-foot-tall, lumpy, blue hulks. Or red-eyed serpents. They're not grandmas who teach algebra. They're bad guys who pop out of portals. Or have you forgotten?"

Hay Lin shuddered. There was no way she could forget how horrible the Metamoorian creatures were. She'd only recently come face-to-face with an enormous blue one in Elyon's basement. She still remembered his yellow fangs and the stony lumps on his head. How could she forget the venom in his beady little eyes as he'd lunged at Hay Lin, trying to drag her into the portal? She would have been a goner if her friends hadn't transformed themselves into their magical forms and slammed in to rescue her.

Hay Lin shook herself out of the memory and gave Mrs. Rudolph another look. The lady was petite and plump, with a wobbly double chin and giant, tinted glasses. She wore a green scarf pinned with a little brooch. She looked as harmless as a house cat.

The teacher smiled warmly as Will handed her a slip of paper. Then she began walking plumply down the sidewalk.

"Let's follow her!" Irma blurted. She ducked around the pillar and began slinking down the sidewalk, half a block behind the maths teacher. Hay Lin trotted along behind Irma.

"I can't believe we're spying on a *maths teacher*, when we could be on our way to the store," she complained.

"Have you forgotten who you are?" Irma

said, giving Hay Lin a sneaky smile. "You're a Guardian of the Veil. Spying on aliens from another world is totally part of the job description."

Hay Lin huffed indignantly. But, as she was sure Irma had known she would, she acquiesced.

"Have it your way, spy girl," she'd said.

The two girls crept along the sidewalk, being careful to stay several ̇ paces behind Mrs. Rudolph. Irma ducked behind a tree, looking over her shoulder with exaggerated furtiveness.

Hay Lin giggled and somersaulted to a crouching position behind a garbage can. Two can play at this "spy game," she thought.

"The coast is clear," Irma hissed. Then the two girls began stealing up the sidewalk again.

This feels just like when we were little, Hay Lin thought with a grin. We'd play Spy, Detective, Policewoman – anything that gave us an excuse to sneak around Heatherfield and duck into places we shouldn't be.

Part of Hay Lin wanted to think of this as just another one of those little-kid games. Something fun. Something light.

But deep down in the pit of her stomach,

she'd known this was serious. Irma might have been joking about Mrs. Rudolph, but the truth was, bad guys from Metamoor *were* out there! Hay Lin had seen them. And now, her old fearlessness was history.

The realisation made Hay Lin shiver. Her stomach growled again and she returned to the present. She was still standing, hungry and miserable, outside Mrs. Rudolph's big pink-granite house. Hay Lin glanced at her watch. They'd been standing there for the past two hours, peering into the maths teacher's window. It had been the most boring two hours of her entire life.

"You want to know Mrs. Rudolph's secrets?" Hay Lin said to Irma in exasperation. "She spends the whole afternoon grading maths tests! Why can't you admit you were wrong?"

Irma shrugged.

"Maybe I will," she said. "But first, I want to check one more time."

"Whatever . . ." Hay Lin muttered.

"I've got an idea," Irma said suddenly. "Are you free tomorrow morning?"

"We are *supposed* to be in school tomorrow morning," Hay Lin said irritably. She started walking away from Mrs. Rudolph's – and towards her apartment.

"Oh," Irma scoffed, falling into step beside Hay Lin. "We'll spend almost twenty years of our life in a classroom. We can take one little day off!"

"Irma!" Hay Lin gasped. "You're terrible. When I get flunked, I'll know who I have to thank."

"What if that woman really is a monster?" Irma protested. "Don't be selfish, Hay Lin. You have a chance to save the world."

"No, no, no," Hay Lin chanted. But inside, she could feel her resistance crumbling. Irma was pressing every one of her buttons – her sense of adventure . . . her hunger to save the world . . . her desire to get out of school whenever she could.

"I don't want to," Hay Lin said weakly.

"Are you *really* going to change your mind?" Irma said, staring at Hay Lin tauntingly.

"Oh, for Pete's sake," Hay Lin sputtered. "You know what? Okay!"

The next morning, there they were, once again holed up behind the wall outside Mrs.

Rudolph's house, surveying the scene.

I cannot *believe* I okayed this, Hay Lin thought miserably.

She and Irma had had to sneak past the school to get here. They'd jumped as the early-morning bell rang. Then they'd skittered nervously down the alleys behind the buildings, hoping not to be spotted by any grown-ups.

And now, they were holding their breath and waiting for Mrs. Rudolph to emerge.

Suddenly, the front door of the pink house opened.

Their target was in sight!

Mrs. Rudolph stepped out onto the porch, wearing a bright pink coat and her woolly green scarf. She locked the front door and slipped the key beneath a pot of pink flowers at the top of the porch steps.

Hay Lin and Irma stood perfectly still as Mrs. Rudolph lumbered down the steps and through the front gate. Then she walked down the block and disappeared around the corner.

"All clear?" Irma whispered to Hay Lin.

Hay Lin gulped. There was still time to make it back to Sheffield. She'd simply get a tardy demerit – no biggie. But one look at

Irma's determined blue eyes and Hay Lin knew there was no backing out now.

"Nobody around," she whispered resignedly.

Irma hopped lightly onto a garbage can and pulled herself up to the top of the wall. As she dropped to the lawn on the other side of the fence, Hay Lin clambered after her.

"I'm sweating," Hay Lin hissed.

"This is the warmest autumn we've had in twenty-five years," Irma said as she started across the lawn. "I heard it on TV."

"You know what I mean," Hay Lin said, pointing a cranky finger at her friend.

"Don't worry!" Irma scoffed. "We'll just do a tiny bit of poking around."

"What'll we do if Mrs. Rudolph comes back?" Hay Lin asked as the girls climbed the steps to the front porch.

"Mrs. Rudolph's at school," Irma assured Hay Lin. "She won't be back for the whole day."

With that, Irma pulled a plastic card out of her jeans pocket. Hay Lin recognised it as her friend's phone card. Irma's dad insisted she carry one with her in case she ever needed to make an emergency call. Being a police sergeant, Mr. Lair was a total worrier.

Irma must have picked up tips about breaking and entering from her dad, too! Hay Lin gaped as Irma slipped the phone card into the cranny between the door and the doorjamb. She started jiggling the card around, trying to unlock the door.

"What are you doing?" Hay Lin asked. "Why don't you just use the key under the flowerpot?"

"This way, we won't have to touch anything," Irma whispered. "We won't leave any trace. It always works in the movies. Look . . ."

Irma jiggled the card some more. She shifted it up and down. Then she scowled and bent the card back and forth.

*Craaaccckk!*

"Oh, no!" Irma cried. Oh, yes. The phone card had snapped in two. She stared at it in horror.

"May I?" Hay Lin said, rolling her eyes. She went to the flowerpot at the edge of the porch and swiped the key out from underneath it. Then she nudged Irma aside, unlocked Mrs. Rudolph's door, and stepped into the house. The foyer was dim, but grand, with a little

Oriental rug, a dramatic, green-carpeted stair-case, and a brass chandelier.

"You first!" Hay Lin said, motioning Irma inside.

"But . . . but . . ." Irma stood on the porch, stuttering nervously. Finally, she stepped into the middle of the foyer.

Hay Lin was feeling more confident now. She could *totally* handle this mission. She could even make sure Mrs. Rudolph wouldn't suspect a thing!

While Irma poked timidly around the foyer, Hay Lin used the key to lock the door from the inside. Then she went to a window next to the door and slid it open.

"And now, just a light breeze," she said playfully. She held the key on her palm. Then she felt her magic well up within her, like a cool gust of wind.

Pursing her lips, Hay Lin blew on the key. Her breath came out as a silvery wisp of magic! It carried the key out the window on a pillow of air. Then it lifted the flowerpot as if it had weighed no more than a pebble. Finally, it slid the key back underneath.

"There!" Hay Lin announced, turning to

Irma triumphantly. "The key is back in place."

"Bright idea!" Irma said. But her tone of voice wasn't exactly nice. In fact, she was scowling at Hay Lin. "Now you've locked us in!"

Oh. Uh, Irma had a point there. Hay Lin's shoulders sagged.

So, I was a *little* impetuous, she thought guiltily. That's just what Dad said to me last night when I finally got home from the stakeout Irma and I had. Maybe I oughtta work on that a bit.

But there was no time to start fixing that now. There was way too much snooping to do. Hay Lin started to follow Irma into Mrs. Rudolph's living room.

"You just stay here," Irma said, holding up her hand. "You've done enough already."

"Okay, okay," Hay Lin said with a grin. She knew Irma couldn't stay mad at her for long. She gave a salute and added, "I'll stand guard. But, hurry up, sir!"

Hay Lin peeked out the front window. As Irma shuffled around in the living room, then the kitchen, she called out, "If only we knew what we were looking for."

"I know," Hay Lin agreed. "It seems like a perfectly ordinary house. So, you're not finding anything?"

"Nothing," Irma said, coming back to the foyer after a few minutes. "Let's try upstairs."

Irma trotted up the stairs with Hay Lin following her.

"Aha!" Irma cried triumphantly as she ducked into a bedroom. When Hay Lin peeked in, she saw a big, comfy-looking bed, an wardrobe, a lot of little pictures on the walls, and other ordinary bedroom stuff.

"Uh, Irma," Hay Lin said dryly. "There's nothing in here."

"I wouldn't call that wardrobe nothing," Irma declared. "Or that chest!"

She pointed to a big trunk at the foot of the bed. Then, with a sneaky smile on her face, she walked over to the wardrobe. In one swift motion, she threw its doors open and began rifling through Mrs. Rudolph's cardigan sweaters and voluminous dresses.

"Irma!" Hay Lin gasped. "What are you doing? You promised we wouldn't touch anything."

"Well . . . I changed my mind," Irma

declared. "C'mon. Help me."

Hay Lin shook her head. She didn't want to stick her nose into Mrs. Rudolph's closet. It smelled like lavender and something else in there. Yuck. Instead, she drifted over to the bedroom window.

Idly, she gazed out over the street below. Adults were strolling busily down the sidewalk. There were businessmen in suits with briefcases, mums with strollers, delivery guys. . . .

So, this is what Heatherfield looks like during school hours, Hay Lin mused. No bicycles, no Rollerbladers, no kids, no . . . way!

"*Eeeek!*" Hay Lin shrieked.

"Aha!" Irma cried, running over to join her at the window. "Did you find something?"

"No, but someone's going to find us!"

Hay Lin pointed with a trembling finger at the house's front gate. Mrs. Rudolph was walking right through it!

# SIX

Irma gasped. She pressed her hands to the window and stared at the woman hauling two heavy shopping bags up the front walk.

"Mrs. Rudolph!" she shrieked. "Wh – what is she doing here? She was supposed to be in school!"

"It's all your fault!" Hay Lin yelled back at her. Then she turned on her heel, dashed out of the bedroom, and sped down the stairs.

Irma careened after her.

"Don't panic! Just don't panic," Irma cried. "I have an emergency plan."

The girls skidded to a halt in the living room. Hay Lin spun around to face Irma.

"What plan?" she demanded. Then she gasped and looked at the front door.

*Thump. Thump. Thump.* That was the sound of Mrs. Rudolph's heavy feet tromping up the stairs to the porch.

*Thump. Thump. Thump.* That was the sound of Irma's heart slamming in her chest.

Irma bit her lip.

What plan, indeed? She had no plan! In fact, it had never even occurred to her that they could be caught. Now, for the first time, something else struck Irma.

Could Mrs. Rudolph *really* be a creature from Metamoor who had somehow sensed the presence of the Guardians in her house?

Were Irma and Hay Lin in actual danger?

Irma couldn't believe it. Really, she'd meant for the whole outing to be an adventure, a magical and fun adventure. Once again, being magical had turned out to be nothing but a big bummer!

Her magic wasn't going to get her out of this fix. No, Irma was going to have to rely on something very, very basic.

"Let's hide!" she whispered. She ran across the living room and threw open a door. Behind it was a small closet cluttered with a few boxes, brooms, and dustpans.

As Mrs. Rudolph's key began to click in the

lock, Hay Lin unleashed a terrified squeak and zipped across the room after Irma. The girls dove into the closet and pulled the door shut. An instant later, Mrs. Rudolph stepped inside the house.

Irma squeezed one eye shut and pressed the other to the closet door. She could just see Mrs. Rudolph through the narrow slit between the door and doorjamb. The teacher's short, straight, blonde hair was sticking to her damp forehead. She dragged her heavy grocery bags over to the coffee table and thunked them down with a moan.

"Ooof," she said, letting go of the heavy bags and straightening up painfully. She pressed her hands to her back.

"*Ouch, ouch, ouch,*" she complained. "Oh dear, my back. It's time I start using the supermarket's delivery service."

Wow, Irma thought, Mrs. Rudolph must be even older than she looks.

Hay Lin was not impressed.

"Here she is," she whispered to Irma tauntingly. "Your *evil* creature from Metamoor. Looks like she's got a bad case of arthritis."

"*Shhh,*" Irma hissed. She peeked through

the door again. "She's making a phone call."

"*Oooh,*" Hay Lin said, wiggling her fingers at Irma. "I'm *so-o-o-o* scared. Maybe she's going to ask a few monsters to tea."

Irma whipped around and glared at Hay Lin.

"Should I pinch you?" she whispered. "Do you want me to pinch you?"

Before Hay Lin could answer, they heard Mrs. Rudolph's voice.

"Hello, Will?" she was saying.

Irma caught her breath and returned to her spying. Mrs. Rudolph was perched on the arm of a chair near the telephone table. "This is Mrs. Rudolph. Do you have a minute?"

Irma glanced at Hay Lin, who looked startled. Then they continued eavesdropping.

"Why don't you come by this afternoon for that tutoring," Mrs. Rudolph said. "Today's my day off. . . . So I'll be waiting for you after school, then?"

After a pause, Mrs. Rudolph nodded.

"Perfect. See you later," she said to Will. Then she hung up.

"Very good," Mrs. Rudolph said, pulling herself to her feet. She went to the coffee table and rifled through one of her grocery bags.

"That means I've got some time to relax," she murmured. "I'll have a nice snack and read a book."

Irma huffed in frustration as she watched Mrs. Rudolph pull a pineapple out of the grocery sack.

That phone call to Will was totally innocent, she thought. And now, we're going to have to sit here in the closet while Mrs. Rudolph reads and eats a healthy fruit snack. At the very least, she could do something funny, like eating peanut butter out of the jar with her fingers. Or jumping around on the bed. Or something else you couldn't *ever* imagine a teacher doing.

Irma almost giggled. But she stopped herself when something else caught her eye through the crack in the closet door. She pressed her face back to the door for a closer look.

Irma's eyes widened. A hot rush of fear washed through her.

Mrs. Rudolph *was* doing something strange. And it was definitely something Irma couldn't imagine a teacher doing.

Their sweet, portly maths teacher was holding her pineapple in her hand. It seemed innocent enough. But instead of going to the kitchen to slice it up, she simply looked at it hungrily and opened her mouth wide.

Her teeth! Irma thought in alarm. Her teeth are as pointy and jagged as a shark's. They're . . . fangs!

Mrs. Rudolph's pointy choppers were sharp enough to rip right through a pineapple's rough skin. And that's just what they did: the teacher took a huge bite right out of the unpeeled fruit.

"Hmmm," Mrs. Rudolph muttered with her mouth full of pineapple chunks. "Very tasty!"

"Oh, no," Irma whispered. She couldn't quite believe what she'd just seen!

"What?" Hay Lin whispered. "What did you see?"

Irma shook her head. She couldn't speak. She wished she were somewhere else – at home, trading jokes with her dad. Or in the bathtub. Or even at school!

Anywhere but here.

Feeling as if she were in a trance, Irma pressed her eye to the crack in the door again.

Mrs. Rudolph had finished devouring her pineapple. Now she was lowering herself painfully down onto a red-velvet armchair. She plunked one of her feet onto a footstool in front of the chair and pulled her high-heeled shoe off.

"These things are killing me," she murmured.

Irma frowned in confusion.

Wait a minute, she thought. Now Mrs. Rudolph looks totally normal. She actually looks like somebody's grandmother in that awful gray skirt and brown sweater.

Was Irma's mind playing tricks on her? Had she imagined the fangs? She watched Mrs. Rudolph settle back into her chair and pick up a book from the table.

Then Mrs. Rudolph started to read.

Irma shrugged.

Huh, she thought. Okay, so it was a false alarm. I'm completely making up stories. But I'm just going to keep spying for a little bit. There's nothing else to do, after all.

Irma continued to peek out at Mrs. Rudolph. A moment later, she uttered a tiny gasp. She *hadn't* been imagining the teacher's pointy teeth. Because now the rest of her was changing, too!

At first, the changes were so subtle Irma almost didn't catch them. But then they became unmistakable – Mrs. Rudolph's feet were morphing from a woman's feet into . . . paws! Monstrous paws, with three floppy toes and thumblike digits sprouting from the heels. They reminded Irma of a sloth she'd seen once in the zoo.

Next, Mrs. Rudolph's hands thickened into horny claws.

Her skin turned green and brown. It looked as leathery as an armadillo's shell.

Most horrifying of all was Mrs. Rudolph's plump face. It made an awful crunching noise as it widened and bulged. The teacher's nose shortened into a snout. Her eyes turned bulgy and bright red. Her ears became long and floppy, almost like soft antlers. And thick, red, dreadlock-type things sprouted from her head. Most grotesque of all was the column of stubby red horns that suddenly jutted from her meaty neck.

Mrs. Rudolph wasn't just a creature from Metamoor. She was an enormous and *disgusting* creature from Metamoor!

Irma felt her hands turn icy. Cold sweat popped out on her forehead. She felt she was going to be sick! Or she might just . . .

"Faint," Irma whispered woozily. "I'm going to faint. . . . Help me, Hay Lin!"

Irma's eyelids fluttered as she collapsed on the floor. She heard her body hit the hard wood with a soft thump. Then she saw Hay Lin's face – pale and anxious – hovering above hers.

"Irma," she whispered. Irma could hear the panic in Hay Lin's voice. She knew all her friend wanted to do was run. And so did Irma! But she was too weak. She could barely keep her eyes open. . . .

"Irma!" Hay Lin begged again. "Wake up!"

All Irma could do was open her mouth in a wordless, soundless scream as she looked over Hay Lin's shoulder. The closet door was slowly opening. And looming in the doorway was the creature formerly known as Mrs. Rudolph. She was as big around as a tree trunk. Her red eyes were sparking with anger.

"May I help you ladies?" the creature growled.

Hay Lin jumped and glanced over her shoulder. Her hand tightened on Irma's arm. Her mouth snapped open in horror. And the last thing Irma heard before everything went black was Hay Lin's squeaky scream: *"He-e-e-e-elp!"*

# SEVEN

Will trudged slowly up the sidewalk toward the address Mrs. Rudolph had given her. She was feeling totally torn. On one hand, she dreaded spending the next hour on maths. On the other, she was grateful to Mrs. Rudolph for taking an interest in her.

"I guess at least *some* grown-ups care about what I think," she muttered to herself.

And then again, some *don't*, she added in her mind. She was thinking, of course, about her mother. Last night had been decidedly uncomfortable. When her mum had gotten back from work, she'd tried to pull Will into a heart-to-heart about "Dean." Before she'd even taken off her coat, she'd come into the kitchen, where Will was still brooding, still not eating her bread and chocolate.

"Honey," her mum had said, reaching for Will's shoulder.

Will had sighed and squirmed out of her mother's reach. So her mum had simply sat down next to her. Morosely, she'd picked up one of Will's slices of bread and opened her mouth to take a bite. But then, just as her daughter had, she'd tossed it back onto the plate.

"I don't know what to say, Will. I've told you the truth," she said.

"Let's just not talk about it," Will muttered through gritted teeth.

"I want you to know," her mum said. "It *was* just a business meeting. But, well . . . after we talked for a while, maybe it did become a little more social."

"Stop!" Will cried, slapping her hands over her ears in disgust.

That had made her mum go all stern and scowly.

"Listen, I'm sorry if I surprised you today," she said. "I'm sorry about everything – all the changes. But the fact is, I'm going to have to move on with my life eventually. And so are you."

Will had given her mother one withering glare and stomped off to her room. She'd slammed the door and flopped onto her bed. Her dormouse scrambled up to perch on top of her stomach. He sniffed at her chin and looked at her quizzically. Will patted the animal's head idly as she fumed.

"*I'm* going to have to move on with my life?" she complained. "If only my mum knew how *much* I've moved on. I've been morphing into this strange magical thing; fighting off ugly bad guys from some unknown world; searching for Elyon; trying to pass maths! And she wants me to move on? Ha! My mother is completely out of touch."

The dormouse had cocked his twitchy little head, then pounced onto her foot to gnaw on her sock. Will had sighed. And, then, she'd stayed in her bedroom, avoiding her mum, for the rest of the night.

This morning, she'd merely waved good-bye to her mother before heading off to school. Her attitude had been so chilly, Will had half-expected icicles to sprout from the loft floor.

The image made Will shiver – from sadness more than cold. Will had thought she could count on her mum through anything. They were supposed to be a team. A team of two. Not two, plus one mustachioed history teacher. He was *not* part of the Heatherfield plan.

Of course, flunking maths isn't part of the plan either, Will thought. So she continued to trudge toward Mrs. Rudolph's big, pink house. She walked up the front steps. It was time to make her entrance.

"Oh, it's you, Will."

Mrs. Rudolph opened the door with a warm smile.

"Please come in, dear," she said. Will thanked her and walked through the foyer into the living room.

Pretty nice house for a maths teacher, Will thought. I wonder where Mrs. Rudolph is fr–

*Thuuump!*

Will jumped! The closet door had just flown open. And inside was–

"Irma!" Will screamed.

Irma was sitting on the floor of the closet. Her legs were tied with ropes and her hands were bound behind her back. A white handkerchief was bound tightly around her mouth. Behind her, Hay Lin huddled against the closet wall. She was bound and gagged, too.

No force could keep Irma quiet for long. As Will stood in the middle of the living room – frozen in fear and confusion – Irma shook her head back and forth. Finally, she squirmed enough to edge the handkerchief out of her mouth. Then she shouted at Will, "It's a trap!"

Will spun around to face Mrs. Rudolph, who was clasping and unclasping her hands nervously before her chest.

"Mrs. Rudolph," Will gasped desperately. "What's going on?"

"I . . . I . . ." the teacher stuttered, "I can explain everything, Will!"

She started to come toward her, her arms outstretched. But Irma screamed again.

"Watch out, Will," she warned. "She's a monster from Metamoor!"

Will was trying to wrap her brain around this bizarre scene. Her two friends were tied up in the closet. And her maths teacher was . . . an alien?

If so, she was an alien who was getting a little too close for comfort. Mrs. Rudolph was making her way across the living room, her face contorted with fear and regret.

Will gazed at her maths teacher. Before she could figure out whether to choose fight or flight, Will's head started to spin. She clutched it with both hands.

She was feeling that familiar dizziness.

And the unpleasant prickles in her skin.

And the cold sweat.

*Uhhnnn,* Will moaned inwardly. Not again! There's something in this house! Or . . . someone . . .

Suddenly, her vision cleared. Mrs. Rudolph was almost upon her! Will's instincts took over.

"Stay away!" she shouted at the trembling woman. She waved her arm at Mrs. Rudolph and unleashed a flurry of pink-tinted magic.

With a metallic clang, the magic formed a sort of glowing screen in the air. It stopped Mrs. Rudolph in her tracks.

"*Aaaahh!*" the woman cried in pain and surprise.

"Quick!" Irma shouted from behind Will. "Untie us!"

With one last angry glance at Mrs. Rudolph, Will spun around and ran to the closet. She dropped to her knees and unknotted the ropes coiled around Irma. Then she freed Hay Lin.

"Okay!" she said, hopping to her feet. Her mind was racing. "Now what?"

There are three of us, she thought. And only one of Mrs. Rudolph. We're smaller and quicker than she is. I bet we could make a break for it and get to the door.

Will spun around, preparing to dash. But then, she saw something that stopped *her* in her tracks.

"*Aaagh!*" she gasped.

*O*-kay, she thought. Change of plans.

Mrs. Rudolph had disappeared.

In her place was one of the most grotesque creatures Will had even seen. And lately, she'd seen quite a few.

The creature was as big around as it was tall. It had red eyes and red dreadlocks. Its body reminded Will of a scaly turtle and its floppy feet made her think of space aliens. Its voice was growly and burbly and . . . female.

"This is how I really look," the creature said, holding out its stubby, scaly arms imploringly. "But please don't be afraid. I won't harm you!"

The creature pointed one of her claws – as yellowed and hard as a horse's hoof – at Will and added, "You're the keeper of the Heart of Candracar. You're the new Guardians of the Veil!"

So, Will thought shakily, who *hasn't* heard about our crazy new identities? And another thing . . .

"Where's Mrs. Rudolph?" she demanded. "What have you done to her?"

Hay Lin grabbed Will by the elbow.

"Wake up, Will!" she screeched. "She *is* Mrs. Rudolph!"

"And she's getting away!" Irma cried.

It was true. The creature, or Mrs. Rudolph, was making a break for it. She was running up the stairs at a surprisingly swift waddle.

"Don't let her get away!" Irma cried, dashing after the monster. Effortlessly, she plunged past Will. All three girls began chasing Mrs. Rudolph up the stairs.

"Why don't you understand?" the creature called over her shoulder. "This is not what it seems! You've spoiled everything!" She reached the top of the staircase and disappeared around a corner.

"After her!" Irma cried.

The girls finished barreling up the stairs and

ran down the hallway – just in time to see Mrs. Rudolph yank open a hatch in the ceiling. She pulled a ladder down to the floor. The ladder made a few complaining creaks as the creature locked it into place, then groaned under her weight as she scrambled awkwardly up the steps.

"She's holed up in the attic," Hay Lin cried.

"Now we've got her," Irma declared.

Will leaped onto the ladder and climbed into the attic, her friends at her heels. She watched Mrs. Rudolph pound across the room, dodging old furniture, dusty boxes, and broken lamps. It looked like any other attic of a big old house.

But as Will had learned by now – looks are often deceiving.

When Mrs. Rudolph reached the far end of the attic, she extended her arms. The wall began to undulate. And shimmer. It danced between solidity and nothingness.

And then, with a great *fwooooosh*, a tunnel formed in the wall. It seemed to be composed of clouds. Or water. Or roiling earth. It seemed like a little bit of everything.

Only one thing was clear. It was formed by magic.

"It's a portal!" Irma screamed as she ran up behind Will. Mrs. Rudolph turned away from the pulsating hole in the wall and gazed at the girls sadly.

"I thought I'd never pass through this portal again," she growled softly. "It seems I was wrong after all. Good-bye, girls."

"Mrs. Rudolph!" Will called out in bewilderment.

But the woman-turned-monster merely stepped through the portal.

"I'm coming back, Metamoor!" she cried.

Then she was gone.

"What are we going to do, Will?" Hay Lin cried.

A short time ago, Will wouldn't have known what to do.

Or she would have racked her brain for a solution.

But now, the magic within her took over. She lifted her hand. It was already humming with power, spewing jets of pink magic through the dusky attic.

She felt her body contract as strength suffused her arms, then her legs, and finally her mind.

Then Will unclasped her fist. The Heart of Candracar was hovering over her palm, glowing brilliantly.

The sight of the shimmery glass orb, cradled in its swirly, silver prongs, made Will gasp out loud with delight. The Heart sent a silvery, round teardrop of magic over to Hay Lin.

Next, it let fly a bobbling blue orb toward Irma.

Each girl experienced a breathless transformation. They were swooped up in a swirl of magic – magic that elongated their limbs and smoothed out their knobby knees and angular elbows. Their faces grew more beautiful, more knowing. Their hair bounced into shiny, perfect waves around their high cheekbones.

And soon, they were standing tall in their purple-and-turquoise uniforms, their opalescent wings fluttering angrily behind them.

Irma peered into the portal. Mrs. Rudolph was still visible. She was running through the tunnel, but the girls' transformation had happened so quickly she hadn't gotten very far.

"Let's move!" Irma cried. "She's getting away."

Will started to comply. But then, an image

of Hay Lin's grandmother flashed in her mind. Will almost felt as if Yan Lin were speaking to her from some ethereal place. Perhaps it was Candracar, the fortress of magic that had given the girls their power. Or maybe the place was just Will's memory.

All Will knew was that somehow, Yan Lin was reminding her of something important: guarding the Veil meant closing the portals and keeping invaders out. The fleeing monster wasn't nearly as important as the tunnel through which she was escaping.

Will called out to Irma.

"Let her go," she ordered. "Let's focus on the portal instead. At my signal . . ."

Will glanced at Hay Lin and Irma out of the corners of her eyes. They were raising their arms in front of them. Silvery sparks of Hay Lin's airy magic were already flashing from her fingernails. And Irma's hands were blurred by her watery power.

"Hit!" Will yelled.

*Esssaaaaak!*

Will watched a jolt of pink magic shoot from the center of her palms. At the same time, Irma unleashed a stream of blue magic, and Hay Lin a stream of silver. The three separate bands danced and coiled around each other until they had combined to create one vivid, purple mass – a veritable freight train of magic.

It hit the portal with a tremendous boom – as loud as a thunderclap.

The portal entrance was engulfed by a cloud of smoke. After an instant of stunned silence, the cloud began rumbling. Gushes of purple magic started to spew from its center. Then the cloud seemed to gather in on itself, pulling as much air from the attic as it could.

Uh-oh, Will thought desperately. It's gonna *blow!*

*Fwooooommmm!*

Will squeezed her eyes shut as the exploding portal hurled her through the air. She flew backwards.

Then she fell to the floor with a thud.

*"Ooof!"* Will grunted.

She pressed her forehead to the floor for a moment, her entire body shaking from the impact – not to mention the wonder – of what she'd just experienced.

She peeked around the attic.

The portal had disappeared! The dusty

beams and mottled-wood paneling of Mrs. Rudolph's attic wall were completely restored.

Will looked at her hands. The graceful, tapered fingers of her other self were gone! Will's own small, short-nailed hands had returned, as had the overalls and sporty pink pullover she'd been wearing when she'd shown up at Mrs. Rudolph's.

Peeking over her shoulder, Will saw Hay Lin's flailing legs – in her flared jeans and her loafers – poking out of an old trunk. And Irma had collapsed on an old chaise lounge and was batting dust out of her blue jacket.

They were back to normal.

And all previous evidence of a portal to Metamoor – not to mention their maths teacher–turned–Metamoorian monster – was gone.

"Phew," Will breathed, blowing a hank of red hair out of her eyes and gazing incredulously at her friends. "Um . . . don't know if you're busy this afternoon, but we've *got* to call an emergency W.i.t.c.h. meeting."

# EIGHT

Taranee was sitting on the edge of Cornelia's bed. Like everything else in her friend's penthouse apartment, the bed was plush. Its headboard and footboard were antiques – carved wood accented with splashes of gold. The duvet was soft and fluffy. The pillows, fluffy and numerous.

But Taranee was far from comfortable. In fact, she couldn't even begin to enjoy those cushy digs. Like everything else in her life, that seemingly normal bedroom felt deceptive. Danger could be lurking in the dustless corners, in the well-stocked closet, even in the innocent-looking backpacks on the floor.

*Am I just being paranoid?* Taranee thought, gazing at her friends' faces. Hay Lin, Irma, and

Will looked decidedly relaxed. Which was weird, because they'd called this emergency meeting at Cornelia's house right after they'd seen their maths teacher morph into some sort of creature from the Metamoorian lagoon. And they'd closed a portal that had sprung up in Mrs. Rudolph's attic.

Those twisted tunnels to Metamoor popped up in the most unassuming places. The school gym. Elyon's basement.

Where's the next one gonna be? Taranee wondered. Maybe right here in Cornelia's bedroom! Maybe in my parents' kitchen! At this point, anything's possible.

Which meant Taranee could feel secure nowhere.

She didn't even completely trust herself! After all, she was still learning her way around her magical power. What if she accidentally set her bedroom on fire while she slept? Or inadvertently torched the next homework assignment that gave her grief? Or worse?

Taranee shook her head in frustration.

Now is not the time to get all freaked out, she told herself. Focus on the meeting.

She sat on her fire-starting fingers and

tuned back in. Irma and Hay Lin were just finishing the story of their crazy day at Mrs. Rudolph's. Will was sitting cross-legged on Cornelia's rug, listening with a bemused smile. Cornelia was pacing in front of the window, scowling as she listened.

"And then, the portal went *poof,* and we went flying!" Irma was saying with a laugh. "When we came to our senses, we weren't magical anymore. But the portal wasn't there anymore, either."

"We are *such* a kick-butt crew!" Hay Lin crowed.

Suddenly, a squeaky little voice filled the room.

"What'd ya do? Rob a candy store?"

The five girls gasped. They turned toward the voice. It had come from Cornelia's bedroom door.

"Lilian!" Cornelia barked.

Taranee covered her mouth with her hand as Cornelia stormed over to her baby sister, who was giggling and peeking around the door. Had Lilian heard anything?

"Get *out!*" Cornelia yelled at the little girl.

"Why can't I stay?" Lilian demanded with a

scowl. She planted her plump little fists on her hips.

"Because you can't!" Cornelia told her. She scooped Lilian up and pushed her out the door with one sweep of her long, slender arms. "Now, go away!"

Lilian stomped out into the hall.

"I bet you're talking about boys," she yelled tauntingly over her shoulder. "I'm gonna tell Mum!"

"What's up?"

Mrs. Hale's voice sounded in the hall now. She must have just come up the stairs.

Great, Taranee thought. I can't believe we have to save the world *and* dodge our parents! Give me a break!

She crowded behind Irma and Hay Lin at the bedroom door to see what would happen next.

What would happen next was some pretty smooth lying. Cornelia was *good*.

"We're doing our homework, Mum," she said breezily as she nudged her sister over to her mother. "Could you lock this little monkey in her cage, please?"

Irma guffawed and Will giggled. But Lilian

stuck out her lower lip and climbed into Mrs. Hale's arms.

"Oh," Cornelia's mum said to the rest of the girls. "They squabble all the time, but they love each other very much. Don't they?" she asked, looking directly at Cornelia.

"I'll love her even more if she can stay away from my bedroom all afternoon," Cornelia replied. Then she waved good-bye to Lilian and pushed her door decisively shut.

"Come on, Lilian," Taranee heard Mrs. Hale say from the hall. "Your sister and her friends have to do their homework. Why don't *we* bake some cookies?"

"*Wheee!*" Lilian cried.

"Phew," Cornelia said, turning back to her friends. "Now, where were we?"

Will walked over to Hay Lin's backpack, which was lying on the floor next to the bed.

"You know," she said, reaching into the pack and pulling out the mysterious blue book they'd found in Elyon's basement. "I have a feeling this book can tell us a lot."

Irma nodded vigorously.

"I think it's time to find out what this whole thing is about," she declared.

The idea made Taranee's knees feel a bit wobbly. She wasn't sure she *wanted* to know what was inside that book. She propped herself weakly against the footboard of Cornelia's bed.

But the other girls gathered around Will with eager faces.

"Even if we don't know our enemies specifically," Taranee said, "one thing is totally obvious. The creatures from Metamoor are among us. We don't know them, but it's clear they know us!" She felt her heart start to beat faster. "So, I'll say it again: We need to keep our eyes open, okay?"

"*Not* okay," Cornelia said, stamping her foot. She was wearing ballet slippers, so it didn't make much of a thump. But Taranee could still feel Cornelia's indignation. "Let me tell you something – I don't want to go on just 'keeping our eyes open.' I need to know!"

Cornelia started pacing again.

"Who are we supposed to be fighting?" she asked. "Who are these monsters? What do they want from us? The Veil . . . Candracar . . . Metamoor . . . they're just names to me. And these magical powers of ours– "

"We'll need them to open this book," Will

said, clutching the book to her chest.

Hay Lin shook her head and adjusted the pink goggles resting on top of her head.

"It's impossible, Will," she said. "I've already tried."

Will sank to her knees and put the book on the floor in front of her. Taranee joined Cornelia, Irma, and Hay Lin as they formed a circle around the tome.

"You tried on your own," Will pointed out to Hay Lin. "This time, we'll try together. Put your hands on it. . . ."

Will rested her palm on top of the book. But before anyone else could touch it, too, something strange happened.

Will's head dropped forward. She cocked an ear, listening to something. Then she spoke softly, her eyes closed.

"Why are you asking?" she said to no one in particular. "Of course, I don't."

Taranee looked at Cornelia. They exchanged a surprised, questioning look. Was Will hearing voices?

Apparently so. And those voices had told Will something. She came out of her trance and spoke to her friends.

"This book's protected by a magic halo," she reported. "Let's release some of our energy and see what happens."

Cornelia shook her head.

"Destroy my bedroom and you'll see what happens!" she said. Taranee knew what they were all thinking: What choice do we have?

If they didn't take a risk, they'd never know anything.

So Cornelia placed a reluctant hand on the book next to Will's hand. Next, Irma put her fingertips on the book. Then, Hay Lin.

Finally, they all looked expectantly at Taranee.

She felt her stomach flutter. Part of her wanted to run away and go home. She wanted to be where it was safe, where her brother would be rocking out to the same surfer-punk music he always listened to, where her mother would be reviewing cases from court and her dad would be getting dinner started in the kitchen.

Okay, if I'm feeling nostalgic for Dad's home cooking, Taranee thought wryly, something's *definitely* wrong.

Taranee shook thoughts of home from her

head and looked, instead, at her new friends. She took in Will's strong, determined face, Hay Lin's excited smile, and Irma's sly smirk, and felt a little better. Even Cornelia's defiant sneer was somehow comforting.

Maybe, Taranee realised suddenly, I'm not as far from home as I think.

So, with a shy smile, she placed her own trembling fingertips on the book.

Almost immediately, a jolt of green magic began to form between the girls' hands. It traveled from finger to finger until a faintly glowing ring hung over the book, like a halo.

Then . . . the book began to tremble.

And then, it did more than tremble. It levitated – floating right off the floor.

Taranee squeaked in surprise. But nobody let go of the book, so she didn't either.

"That's it," Will whispered. "Be careful now. Don't worry . . ."

Of course, that's exactly when something worrisome happened. The green halo swirling around the book started to swirl a little faster. Then even faster.

In fact, Taranee thought, you could definitely call that a whirl. A *sparking* whirl.

It was true – jolts of starry light were shooting out of the halo. Staticky, zapping noises filled the room.

Next, the green circle began to turn conical. It was a miniature tornado. It carried the book right out of the girls' reach, lifting it toward the ceiling.

"It worked!" Hay Lin breathed. "Something's happening."

"Oh," Taranee gasped, unable to say much else.

For a moment, the girls just stared up at the book as it hovered beneath Cornelia's ceiling. Their mouths hung open. Taranee was sure she could hear the thumping of five hearts in the room. But maybe that was just her own heart, beating five times as hard as usual.

And then, Irma pointed at the trembling tome.

"It's opening!" she cried.

Will jumped to her feet, but Cornelia grabbed her.

"Don't get too close," she warned.

As if Cornelia had predicted it, the book began to sink back towards them. At the same time, the cover continued to open. A few pages flipped back. And then, the book alighted in front of the girls' frightened faces, assaulting them with a surge of acid-green light.

"*Aaah!*" Will cried. Taranee recoiled in terror.

A moment later – when the girls realised none of them had been vapourised, or even burnt, by the tremendous flash – they peered at the book more curiously. The light subsided a bit. And then it died down to a gentle glow.

Taranee blinked the spots out of her eyes and looked at the volume.

"Look at that!" Cornelia exclaimed. "It's not a real book!"

She was right. The book was a container of sorts.

On its right-hand side, where there should have been pages, there was merely a cushion with a cavity cut out of its middle. Nestled inside that cavity was an object.

It looked like a piece of jewelry – a big pendant or pin. The body of the pendant was glazed with brilliant paint – half of the circle was green, the other half white. On top of the circle was a tall, skinny triangle. And on the bottom, a slightly smaller triangle.

It was clearly some kind of symbol. It also

looked . . . awfully familiar.

Suddenly, Taranee recognised it.

That design had been on the floor of Elyon's basement, she realised. It was on the pathway to the portal!

Then Taranee noticed something on the left-hand side of the book. Filling the top half of the page was a series of strange shapes. They were pictures or hieroglyphics or . . .

Taranee leaned in closer. She felt her fear melt away from her, like a fever that had suddenly broken. Now she was merely curious. Those strange letters were intriguing. . . . She *had* to get a closer look.

"There's an inscription here," she murmured to her friends. "A mysterious alphabet . . ."

Taranee leaned in even closer.

"Don't touch it!"

That was Cornelia, warning Taranee away from the inscription. But the warning merely echoed around Taranee's head and disappeared with a poof.

She couldn't help herself. She had to reach out and . . .

*Ding . . .*

"She touched it," Cornelia said, incredulous.

Taranee barely heard her. Her head was too full of the ghostly music that had erupted the moment she touched the book. Actually, it wasn't quite music. It was clangs and chimes and drums and cymbals that had somehow been warped and distorted.

The music subsided quickly – to make way for a voice. A man's voice.

"Fear the name of the prince of Metamoor," the deep voice said. "Kneel down before his shadow."

"Oh!" Taranee cried. She looked up at the ceiling, then glanced wildly around the room. Who was speaking?

"This is the Seal of Phobos," the disembodied voice boomed. Taranee's eyes bulged in fear. But even more frightening was the casual reaction of her friends. They were still staring at the book with expressions of calm curiosity.

"Didn't you hear that?" Taranee gasped. "That voice!"

"What voice?" Hay Lin asked with a shrug.

Taranee felt her head start to spin.

"*That* voice," she said, pointing to the

strange amulet nestled in the book. "The book talked to me. That's the Seal of Phobos."

The other girls blinked at Taranee with blank expressions on their faces. Then Irma made a sudden grab for the amulet.

"I have no idea who this 'Fabius,' is," she said, "but I'd be happy to take care of him now!"

As Irma started to lift the Seal from the book, the voice boomed again in Taranee's head. This time it was so loud she was sure her eyeballs jangled back and forth as a result.

"*Phobos!*" it roared.

"*Ow!*" Irma cried at the same time. She yanked her hand away from the Seal. "It burned me!"

Next, the Seal did more than that. It erupted from the book with a puff of smoke and began to shoot towards the ceiling. It floated in a bubble of blackness.

"Uh-oh," Irma said tremulously as the girls cowered beneath the pulsing amulet. "Did I do something wrong?"

"I knew it!" Cornelia yelled. "That thing is going to destroy my room."

And it is going to take us right along with it, Taranee thought in terror.

That's when the Seal of Phobos began to spew forth a torrent of sludgy, black clouds. The gunky-looking stuff began to creep across the ceiling, as if it were gathering strength for an attack.

*Whoooooosh!*

The black stuff was on the verge of exploding! It quickly doubled in volume, covering the ceiling. Then it hurtled downwards, ready to consume the five girls. It was going to smother them!

"*Eeeek!*" Taranee heard Irma cry.

And then, Will spoke. But her order did *not* inspire a whole lot of confidence.

"Duck!" she screamed!

# NINE

*Duck,* Will thought. Did I really say that? Great. *Brilliant* idea, Will.

Nevertheless, she *did* duck, falling to the floor and covering her head with her hands.

Just a few hours ago, she'd had this same feeling. She'd had a hard time believing that Mrs. Rudolph had turned into a turtlelike ghoul, even though the evidence had been right before her eyes.

Will's mind was grappling with the *current* chain of events. A pretty pendant – a harmless-looking geometric bauble with a green-and-white center – had suddenly sprung to life.

But it can't *really* be spewing black gunk all over Cornelia's bedroom, Will said to herself. Can it?

Fearfully, she peered up at the ceiling through her splayed fingers.

Um, that would be a yes, she thought. This is really happening!

The Seal of Phobos was hurling forth clouds of inky sludge. The stuff was like night air that had become three-dimensional, darkness that had come to life.

And it was clearly evil.

For a moment, all five girls simply stared – stunned – at the roiling, expanding blackness.

But that moment didn't last long. As the blackness began to creep down toward them, Hay Lin screamed. Then she cowered on the floor, crying, "I never thought I'd miss those boring afternoons when we really *were* doing homework!"

Meanwhile, Cornelia dashed across the room. She grabbed the doorknob with both hands and began pulling on it.

"The door's stuck," she cried. "We're locked in!"

"What *is* this stuff?" Taranee wailed.

As Will watched the darkness undulate, growing inkier and denser by the second, a number of possible answers flashed through her mind.

It's evil that's taken form, she thought. It's out to get us.

Or it's some bizarre new baddie from Metamoor that's out to get us.

Or maybe it's our fear. Our fear has become something real, something solid, something that's out to get us.

Will shook her head. Why was she even trying? She didn't have a clue as to what the sludgy stuff was. But she was right about one thing. It was definitely out to get them!

And it was encroaching fast. While Will had been racking her brains for an explanation, the dark gunk had tumbled down the walls and crept across Cornelia's floor. The furniture had become cloaked in it. The girls' feet were lost in it.

Before they knew it, the stuff had climbed up to their waists. It would take only a minute for the blackness to engulf them completely!

As the blackness swirled around her torso, Will watched Hay Lin scream and claw at the wall, trying to escape. But the tarlike darkness wouldn't let her go. Taranee's hands seemed to be caught in the stuff. No matter how hard she pulled, they wouldn't come out. She was stuck!

"Will!" she screamed.

The sound of her name, spoken so desperately by her friend, brought a surge of energy to Will's limbs. She tried to jump out of the sludge. She could feel her leg muscles strain. She could feel her toes stretch and spring.

Will couldn't move. The blackness was up to her rib cage by now and it had her in its grip. In fact, it seemed to be pulling at her with greedy, sucking gulps. Will shook her head back and forth as she struggled to move through the darkness. But that only made things worse! The blackness grabbed her flailing arms and pulled them down to her sides. It had her pinned.

She was helpless.

She was no leader.

As if to prove her point, the blackness suddenly flung itself over her head. It covered her face like a gauzy, oppressive scarf. It draped itself over her eyes. It filled her head.

Will couldn't see Cornelia's room anymore. She couldn't see her own hands, pinned to her sides.

And more importantly, she couldn't see her friends. They'd been swallowed by the inky evil. They'd as good as disappeared.

Will let out a choked sob and wilted. The strength drained from her legs. Her lungs quit their panicked heaving. Her head hung in defeat.

It was all too much.

I can't fight anymore, she thought. I can't do this alone.

Will could think of nothing else until . . . she felt something move in her hand!

At first, it felt like almost nothing – a twitching muscle, or a slight shifting of the sludge.

But then, the thing grew more insistent. It forced Will's fingers to fight the blackness and close into a fist. She felt a sort of warm, pulsing pressure shoot through her entire hand. By the time she sensed jolts of energy shooting up her arm, she knew what had happened.

It was the Heart of Candracar! It was speaking to her from inside her body. And now, it was emerging from her palm. It was reminding Will of her power, her magic.

"Heart of Candracar," Will said suddenly. Her voice made no sound. The moment it left her mouth, it was swallowed up in the blackness. Will persisted.

"We're in danger," she told the Heart. "Please, help us!"

Will bit her lip in hope. She opened her hand to release the orb. And then she peered desperately into the blackness.

It was eerily silent. As dark as a starless night.

Will blinked. Had she seen something?

The darkness was retreating. Will saw a pin-prick of light floating somewhere in the darkness.

The light began growing. Before long, the hole in the blackness was fist-sized. Shafts of brilliant light spilled through it. It pushed back the darkness like a willful bird, struggling to break from its shell.

All four girls seemed to be gravitating closer and closer to her. Finally, Will felt them touching her. They all sank to the floor and huddled together. Will was surrounded by a wall of friends, and, in their center, the Heart of Candracar glowed and pulsed and finally exploded.

The blackness blew into a thousand pieces that flew toward every corner of the room. Then, just as quickly as it had arrived, the darkness evaporated.

Will heaved a sigh of relief. But the feeling didn't last. When she glanced up at Cornelia's ceiling, she realised that, while the blackness might have disappeared, its source remained.

The Seal of Phobos continued to float above them, nestled in a small cloud of blackness.

The Heart of Candracar wasn't going to let it just stay there. It rose from Will's palm up toward the ceiling. The Heart and the Seal hovered next to each other, poised for battle. It was a standoff between light and dark, Candracar and Metamoor, good . . . and evil.

Evil had nothing with which to fight its battle but the Seal.

But good had the Heart of Candracar *and* the five Guardians.

Will rose to her feet. She stood directly beneath the glowing Heart.

Wordlessly, her friends formed a circle around her. It was as if they, too, knew instinctively what to do.

Slowly Will felt something warm well up in ·her chest. It felt like joy or hope. It was the feeling she had whenever she made a new friend, or won a swim meet; when her mother arrived home from a long business trip; whenever life was at its best and sweetest.

And now, it filled Will with peace. She closed her eyes and relaxed into the joy. She felt it grow and grow within her until the feeling burst from her chest. It emerged as a shaft of light.

When Will opened her eyes, she saw that shafts of golden energy were also emanating from the hearts of her friends. The beams rose upward and joined together in a blinding halo around the Heart of Candracar.

They were feeding the heart – filling it with their magic.

And together, they were conquering the Seal of Phobos. With an angry *fzzzzz-ZAAPPP!* the Seal rushed straight toward the Heart. Instead of shattering the delicate glass sphere, the Seal plunged into it. The Heart of Candracar had completely consumed the amulet. In the next moment, the blue book that had held the Seal shot into the Heart as well.

Just like that, the magic disappeared. The Heart of Candracar swooped back into Will's body with a little *thwip*. The girls each slumped to the floor and exhaled in exhaustion.

Will watched Hay Lin flick a bead of sweat from her forehead. Irma rubbed her eyes blearily. But Cornelia looked at the door in alarm. Will followed her gaze.

The door was opening!

What now? Will wanted to scream. *What horrible thing has Metamoor cooked up for us this time? Enough already!*

A blonde head popped into the room, well below the doorknob. Lilian! The little girl's mouth was smeared with chocolate and her blue eyes were scrunched into two mischievous slits.

"I bet you were talking about boys!" Lilian announced. She slammed the door and disappeared. Will could hear her little feet thumping down the hallway.

Will's racing heart began to slow. She looked at her friends wearily.

"Uh," Cornelia groaned. "*That* was definitely worse than maths homework."

"I don't know about you," Irma added. "But after that ordeal, I need a snack!"

"Or at least a change of scenery," Cornelia said, lurching shakily to her feet. "Let's get some air!"

"And sunlight!" Hay Lin piped up. She slung her pink-and-purple backpack onto her shoulder and said, "Let's go."

The girls trooped downstairs, stopping in the kitchen for iced tea and a plate of the cookies Lilian and Mrs. Hale had made. Then Cornelia pointed to the balcony off the kitchen.

"There's plenty of air out there," she said with a smile. "What's more, it's fifteen stories up, and Lilian is afraid of heights!"

"A sister-free zone?" Taranee asked with a smile. "I'm there."

The girls carried their munchies through the sliding glass door, then sank gratefully into the comfy patio chairs on the balcony. Will leaned back into her creaky chair and took a deep, long breath of salty air. The ocean was only a couple of blocks away from Cornelia's building. There were even seagulls flying nearby.

All Will wanted to do was talk about going to the beach. Or boys. Or the horrible Sheffield Institute gym uniforms. Anything but what she was about to talk about.

"Listen," she said wearily. She picked up a cookie and turned it around in her fingers without taking a bite. "I can't explain what just happened. But it does tell us one thing. We found that book in Elyon's basement. There's definitely a link between Metamoor and Elyon's house. What we don't know is if Metamoor and Elyon's family are linked, too."

Cornelia stared at Will with a clenched jaw. Will knew Cornelia still didn't want to believe that her best friend, Elyon, could have had anything to do with Metamoor or, worse, come from there.

"That book doesn't prove anything," Cornelia said. "It could have been in that basement for ages."

"Right," Hay Lin said, jumping in. "Maybe Elyon and her parents were just unlucky and . . . they moved into a haunted house! Like the ones you see in the movies."

Taranee walked to the edge of the balcony and leaned on the railing. She gazed wistfully out at the squawking seagulls.

"I think this whole town is haunted," she announced. "A portal inside the gym. Another in Elyon's house. And a third in Mrs. Rudolph's attic . . ."

"And there are nine other portals," Hay Lin pointed out. She reached into her backpack and pulled out a yellowed, dusty scroll of paper. She unfurled it on the wicker coffee table.

"Oh, right," Cornelia said, rolling her eyes. "We were forgetting your wonderful map."

Will eyed the map. It had been Yan Lin's last gift to her granddaughter before she had died. But it was more than an heirloom. It was a detailed, overhead view of Heatherfield, complete with all the portals to Metamoor – well, the three portals that they'd already found, that is. Each time the girls happened upon a portal, its location on the map took on a pulsing red glow.

"It's the most useless thing in the world," Irma cracked. "The only map that shows you something *after* you've found it."

Will sighed in agreement. But Hay Lin was optimistic as always.

"There must be a good reason, if Grandma gave us this map," she said.

Hay Lin turned to Irma, with expectation and just a little challenge in her playful almond-shaped eyes.

"Or maybe, Irma," she said, "you know the answer."

Irma said nothing. She looked as though she had no clue.

Will felt that since she was the leader, she

should know what to do. She was about to shrug off the whole "leader" thing, but before she had the chance, the Heart of Candracar spoke for her. She felt its power throbbing in her palm and, without thinking twice, she held her hand out toward her friends.

There – once again – was the pulsating glass orb. It floated easily out of Will's palm.

Practise makes perfect, Will thought, as she watched the medallion levitate toward the coffee table. I wonder if the Heart of Candracar is feeling as weary as I am.

She steeled herself for another mysterious message from the glowing object. When it halted over the map and spat a pink flash down onto it, Will gasped.

For the first time ever, the Heart didn't present the girls with a mystery, but with a destination.

A house on the elaborate map began to glow a brilliant red.

"That's Elyon's house!" Will cried. Then she looked around at her friends. And this time, she didn't see indecision or fear. They were each nodding with resignation.

"The message," Will said, nodding in agreement with their silent decision, "is clear."

# TEN

It was time for the Oracle's meditation. He floated through the corridors of his home, the Temple of Candracar. The temple floated, too. It was nestled in silvery, ethereal clouds, in a place where night never fell.

That didn't mean the Oracle never saw evil. On the contrary, he saw all the evil in the world. He also saw all the good. *And* he saw the fragile Veil that separated the two.

In those moments of contemplation, he also saw the Veil's Guardians – the five young girls he had chosen to close the perforations in that gossamer Veil.

Those were the humans whose final destiny was to save the world.

As he came to a halt in his favourite chamber

of the temple – a room containing a perfect, turquoise lily pool – the Oracle closed his eyes. He folded his legs gracefully beneath him. His white, silken robes fell in smooth folds around his knees.

He saw the Guardians gathering in a room. It belonged to Cornelia, the angry one with the yellow hair. She was still fighting her magic. But the Oracle knew that, in her heart, she was beginning to embrace it.

She will have to, he thought with a small smile.

He watched the girls open the book of Phobos. The Seal emerged from the book. As the Oracle witnessed the ensuing battle, his own muscles contracted. He felt the magic that surged through the keeper of the Heart of Candracar. He felt the leader finding her power, her confidence. He felt every emotion and every bit of energy that she felt as she fought off the blackness of Phobos.

The battle ended as quickly as it had begun. The Heart usurped the place of the Seal of Phobos.

The Oracle opened his eyes and smiled.

He had not been wrong about those little

ones, with their rubber-soled shoes and pink-and-purple clothes. He knew that some members of his congregation had feared the girls' youth, their weaknesses, their affection for boys, their attachments to their families.

*Up here in Candracar, we have forgotten,* the Oracle thought, *that in the messiness of humanity, there is a source of strength. Humans call it love.*

*That's something Luba, for instance, would never understand,* the Oracle thought with a chuckle. *I can feel her storming her way through the temple hallways right now.*

When the Oracle cocked his head, he could hear her too.

"Get out of the way," she snarled. "Let me through!"

The Oracle closed his eyes and envisioned Luba's long, silvery pelt, the pointy ears that jutted from her head like the fronds of some exotic plant, and her feline face, which wore a permanent expression of indignation.

Luba was the protector of the Guardians' magic. Today, she had been quite busy. The girls had faced many foes. But none like the challenges that awaited them.

The Oracle had known that that would trouble Luba. She was a loyal congregation member, but an anxious one – always quick to see dangers and mishaps. She didn't have the Oracle's vision.

She was determined, however, to have the Oracle's ear.

"I must talk to the Oracle!" she demanded.

She was blocked by Tibor, the Oracle's adviser.

"This is not the right moment," he barked at Luba. An ancient man, with a four-foot-long beard and white mane, Tibor was nevertheless as strong as a bear. His sole purpose was to stand sentinel behind the Oracle, protecting the Oracle's peace.

It's as if he and I were one person, the Oracle mused. Tibor is the body, a brawny, stalwart presence. And I am the mind – mysterious and weightless.

The Oracle's small body was so light, in fact, that he had levitated right off the ground as he meditated. With his legs still tucked beneath him, he was now floating over the lily pool, enjoying the fragrant breezes wafting off the water.

Thus he was untroubled by Luba's impudence. But Tibor didn't know that.

"The Oracle can't see you right now," the adviser insisted.

But Luba tossed a jolt of magic energy at Tibor. The gesture's impertinence startled Tibor so that Luba was able to push past him, muttering, "That remains to be seen."

"Stop!" Tibor called after her.

But the Oracle held up his hand.

"Let her in, Tibor," he said.

Then, without turning around to face Luba's angry, yellow eyes, the Oracle continued to speak to his adviser.

"I already know Luba's thoughts," he said quietly. "And Luba already knows my answer."

The Oracle felt Luba crouch to the floor, placing her claws beseechingly on the edge of the lily pool.

"This must not be, Oracle!" she cried. "The Guardians are not ready yet! They are still too inexperienced!"

"What you are saying is true," the Oracle allowed with a serene nod of his head. "But it must be. I cannot do anything about it."

"That is not true!" Luba insisted. "You can stop them if you want. You must!"

"What impudence," Tibor gasped as he stole up behind Luba. He glared down at her disapprovingly.

Luba shot Tibor a defiant glare and said, "Should they fail, the Veil will remain without *any* protection against Phobos."

The Oracle closed his eyes. Ah, Phobos. The Guardians had now gotten their first glimpse of the dark Metamoorian prince. His Seal and its darkness had almost conquered them. But the Heart of Candracar had prevailed. Even the Oracle had uttered a sigh of relief when the quiet, red-haired girl had willed the Heart into the darkness, when the Power of Five had shattered the Seal's tremendous strength.

"Those girls are brave, Luba," the Oracle said to his distraught servant. "Try to understand them. Ten thousand years ago, you, too, were as young as they are now."

And as vulnerable, the Oracle added inwardly. Luba wasn't wrong to worry about the Guardians. That was her duty. Everyone had a duty to perform in the face of the certain peril that lay in front of him or her.

# ELEVEN

I can't believe we're going back to Elyon's house, Cornelia thought, with a small groan. She and the other girls had left her apartment building immediately after the Heart of Candracar had illuminated Hay Lin's map. Now they were trudging across town toward Elyon's eerie, abandoned house.

Let's see, Cornelia mused, looking up at the increasingly grey, dusky sky as she walked. The last time we paid a social call to Elyon, she turned into some kind of strange, empty-eyed ghost. She melted through a wall in her basement and enticed us down a dank, brick-lined tunnel. Then the bricks came to life and tried to bury us alive. And to top it all off, Elyon introduced Hay Lin to her new best friend, a huge, blue meanie who tried to drag Hay Lin through a portal to Metamoor.

It's getting harder and harder to remember a time when *I* was Elyon's best friend, Cornelia thought wistfully.

The mystery surrounding Elyon's disappearance was still gnawing at her, like a cut that refused to heal. She still wouldn't allow herself to believe that Elyon had knowingly gone to Metamoor, that she was really the one who was luring Cornelia and her friends into danger.

Maybe we'll finally find some answers here, Cornelia thought as the girls arrived at Elyon's house. They paused for a moment inside the front gate. Unraked leaves skittered around the unkempt and neglected yard. The windows in the house were dark. The newspapers piled high on the front porch were damp and yellowed with age.

Everything about the abandoned building seemed to broadcast a warning: stay away.

I'd love to stay away, Cornelia thought, looking up at the forbidding house. This is about the last place I want to be. But when Hay Lin's map says jump, we jump. Just as when some anonymous elders in some imaginary place called Candracar tell us to save the world, we just agree. We change into magical form, no questions asked.

And my friends just *accept* it all, Cornelia thought indignantly. She shot a sullen glance at Hay Lin, Irma, Will, and Taranee. Maybe *they* don't mind taking orders. But *I'm* used to being the one who makes decisions about my life – what to do after school, whom to hang out with, what cool new clothes to buy.

Now, she thought bitterly, those days are over. I have to follow the herd, or at least, Will. I just hope she's up to leading us.

Actually, that's exactly what Will was doing just then. She was the first one to tromp across Elyon's overgrown lawn and climb the stairs to the front porch. As she placed a firm hand on the front doorknob, Taranee whispered, "This place gives me the shivers."

Will nodded in agreement.

"I don't like it either," she admitted. "But it's the only clue we have to find out what happened to Elyon."

Solemnly, Cornelia and the others followed Will into the stale-smelling, echoey house. They tiptoed across the living room to the unassuming door under the stairs. Then they descended the curving staircase into the creepy, circular basement. Just as it had the last time she had been there, the room reminded Cornelia of a giant tin can. Its walls were made of curved, metal slabs. The floor was stubbly, gray cement. The boxes and bicycle propped up beneath the stairs looked even more lonely and dusty than they had the first time.

The one thing that was different was the huge gash in the wall opposite the stairs. Cornelia stared at the jagged hole. It was hard to believe that she was responsible for it; but she was. She'd flung her arms out and assaulted the wall with waves of green magic. She'd literally moved the earth to help her friends discover the tunnel deep beneath Elyon's house.

Cornelia couldn't help but smile proudly as the girls once again stepped through the doorway she'd created.

Slowly they began walking through the tomb-like tunnel. It was damp and chilly. The yellow lights on the wall cast a dingy glow over everything. Even Cornelia's pretty, pink shawl and long, purple skirt looked worn and droopy there.

"Here we are again," Irma sighed. Nodding, Cornelia looked up at the arches that divided the tunnel into sections.

"Now what?" Irma asked.

"There must be a reason the Heart of Candracar led us here," Will declared. So the girls walked on in silence.

I'm glad *she* has so much faith in that little piece of glass, Cornelia thought sourly. Me, I'm not so sure.

And clearly, she wasn't the only one. Suddenly, Taranee's frightened voice broke through the gloomy, silent air.

"Listen!" she shrieked to her friends. "Listen!"

Cornelia cocked her head and looked warily at Will, Hay Lin, and Irma. They all looked totally perplexed.

"Um, Taranee," Cornelia said gently. "We can't hear anything."

But Taranee ignored her. Her eyes were bulging with fear and her hands were clenched and trembling.

"It's the same voice!" she insisted. "It's whispering a name: Phobos! Over and over."

That's when the Heart of Candracar made

another surprise appearance. It popped out of Will's palm, glowing insistently. The girls peered at it. Inside its pulsating glass orb was the distinct shape of the Seal of Phobos. Its circular emblem and pointy ends were distorted by the sphere, but it was definitely still there.

"What can we do?" Irma wondered. "The Seal's inside the Heart."

"And it oughtta stay there," Hay Lin said determinedly.

Cornelia shivered. Hay Lin was right. It would be a long time before she could forget what that Seal had done to her bedroom.

But Will was gazing trustingly at the Seal locked inside the medallion.

"The Heart of Candracar always knows what's right," she said.

"Oh, please!" Cornelia blurted out suddenly. She had so had it with following a silly necklace all over Heatherfield. "I don't like this at all. I don't want that thing to tell me what to do."

The other girls – even more freaked-out than Taranee – stared at Cornelia in surprise. It was as if she'd committed some terrible blasphemy or something. Why couldn't they see how ridiculous this situation was?

"True," Cornelia continued. "The Heart got us out of trouble. But one day, it could fail to do that. It could . . . I don't know . . . its energy could run down."

As Cornelia folded her arms stubbornly across her chest, she heard Hay Lin say something to Irma. Cornelia spun around just in time to catch the last snatch of her whisper.

"Can I turn her into a crow now?" Hay Lin was asking her friend.

"Nobody would notice the difference anyway," Irma replied with a giggle.

"I heard that!" Cornelia said, bearing down on Irma. "Why don't you tell me what you think to my face?"

Cornelia clenched her fists and braced herself for a retort. Irma always had a wisecrack in her pocket. Especially for Cornelia.

Well, maybe not *always*. In fact, right now, Irma was speechless. Her lips quivered and the only quip she could manage was *"Eeep!"*

Cornelia laughed.

"Oh, what's wrong, Irma? Are you *afraid* of me?" she asked snidely. "Well, at least you're not making fun of me anymore."

"I– I'm not afraid of you," Irma said. "I'm afraid of what's behind you!"

Cornelia gaped at Irma. *What–*

Then she spun around.

*"Aaaahhh!"* Cornelia screamed.

"The portal," Taranee cried from somewhere behind Cornelia. "It's open again!"

Tell me something that's *not* painfully obvious, Cornelia thought, desperately. She fell to her knees and clutched at the cold, stone floor. The portal had erupted from the wall, spewing stone and bricks all around Cornelia's head. The mouth of the tunnel was ringed with silvery, swirling vapour. And inside, Cornelia could see the same throatlike ridges she'd spotted in the corridor that had led them here. The ridges were contracting and rolling, like an animal trying to swallow its prey.

And the prey? She was it! Cornelia was closest to the portal. She could feel it trying to pull her in, with powerful, greedy gulps. She clawed at the floor, trying to resist the pressure.

"Hang on!" Hay Lin cried to Cornelia. Irma and Taranee stared at her in horror.

It seemed that Will had eyes only for the Heart of Candracar, which was still floating above her palm. The Heart was shooting spears of silvery magic toward the portal. Cornelia cringed as the magic whizzed by her head. She was surprised it wasn't setting her hair on fire.

But the Heart wasn't targeting Cornelia. It was focused on the portal. Shafts of magic extended between the orb and the tunnel, linking the two with a sort of magical net.

"I think I've got it!" Will cried, over the roar of the swirling portal. "The Seal of Phobos is the key to entering Metamoor!"

Will gulped and looked at Cornelia. Will's brown eyes flashed at her. In them, Cornelia saw a spark of adventure, a flicker of fear, and a whole lot of determination.

"Are you thinking what I'm thinking?" Will asked.

Cornelia glanced over her shoulder at the predatory portal. It seemed to be sucking at her harder, now. She longed to have enough power to fight it off.

And that power could only come from one thing.

Narrowing her eyes, Cornelia turned back to Will and nodded.

Immediately, Will threw back her head and

thrust her palm out toward her friends. Cornelia gasped as she watched the Heart of Candracar explode in a rainbow of lights. A watery, blue teardrop shot toward Irma and whirled around her, replacing her jeans and pale blue jacket with a tiny purple skirt, springy, striped leggings, and a pair of iridescent wings.

A silvery *whoosh* enveloped Hay Lin, transforming her into an elfin, airborne blur.

The Heart's pink magic infused Will, rounding out her skinny torso and lengthening her arms and legs.

Taranee's bright-orange teardrop changed her fearful expression into one of sheer, fiery ambition.

Finally, Cornelia felt her own shimmery, green teardrop swirl around her like a mossy cloak. It whisked around her and bathed her in the scents of damp earth and freshly cut grass.

Cornelia threw her arms above her head as her W.i.t.c.h. clothes appeared on her body. She loved the long, swirly, purple skirt, the midriff-skimming top and the supple boots that hugged her calves as if they had been custom-made just for her.

Most of all, she loved the wings that had sprouted painlessly from her back. She could feel them fluttering in her hair, which was longer and silkier than it had been before. The ticklish feeling would have made her laugh out loud if this had been a happy transformation.

But it wasn't.

The girls had turned into their magical forms, so that they could plunge into the portal. And on the other side of that pathway was Metamoor – a place filled with unknowns.

"Okay," Will said, glancing at her witchy crew. "We're ready!"

*Whooooooshhh!*

As Will spoke, the mouth of the portal erupted into hot, angry flames.

"Maybe not," Will said.

"Oh, brother," Cornelia complained. She'd been just about to hop into the tunnel. She would have been smoked in a second!

"Are we supposed to jump through that ring of fire?" Irma demanded, backing away from the crackling tunnel. "Forget it! I'm not working in a circus."

Will looked at Taranee.

"Well," Will said with a shrug, "these aren't

your usual sort of flames. But your powers might work anyway. It's worth another trip."

Cornelia saw Taranee bite her lip for just an instant. Will and Taranee exchanged an empowering glance. It reminded Cornelia of Elyon. They'd had a bond like that between Will and Taranee – a sort of silent, best-friend language.

The thought made Cornelia want to see her friend more than ever.

But, she wondered as she stared at the ring of flames, is the risk too great?

She didn't have much time to ponder the question. Taranee was gearing up for action.

"Well," she said to Will, "I guess we're about to find out what my powers can do."

She braced her purple boots on the stone floor and held her hands out in front of her. As orange bursts of magic flowed from her palms, Taranee scowled at the fiery tunnel.

"Do you hear me?" she shouted at the fire. "Get out of the way!"

*SSSsssssssszzzzttt.*

"Wow!" Taranee gasped. "It did what I told it to!"

Cornelia gasped. The fire had indeed disappeared the instant Taranee had issued her order. After the flames fizzled out, the portal seemed to cough a little, expelling a wan puff of smoke. And then it was still. No fire. No steamy swirls of air. No pulsating walls.

It was just an ordinary, brick-lined tube leading to . . . who knew where.

"Come on!" Will said, running towards the opening in the wall. "Let's go!"

"Wait a minute!" Cornelia cried suddenly. "What happens if we get stuck on the other side?"

Will shrugged and tapped her palm.

"We have the Seal of Phobos," she said. "If it worked to get us in, it'll also work to get us out."

Cornelia gaped at Will.

"You make it seem as if you'd known these things all your life," Cornelia spat. "Little Miss I-Know-Best!"

Cornelia saw Hay Lin and Irma exchange irritated glances. Will merely smiled at Cornelia.

"You're right," she said quietly. "But something tells me it will work."

"And maybe Elyon is on the other side," Irma piped up. "That's enough of a reason to go. Don't you think?"

"Right," Will declared. "Now who's coming with me?"

Cornelia scanned her friends' faces. They were all looking at their leader. Will's usual sheepish smile was gone. Instead, her forehead was furrowed with determination and her mouth was twisted into a rakish smile. She was ready for this mission, no matter what it held.

Well, Cornelia thought defiantly, if she's ready, *I'm* ready.

With that, she followed Will into the portal.

The girls crept along the brick pathway. Cornelia felt off balance on the curved floor. She supported herself against the walls as she moved through the tunnel.

Soon a left turn popped up. Cornelia couldn't help but feel glad that Will had been the first one to peek around the corner.

But there was nothing there. The tunnel just continued on.

After a little while, the girls came to another corner. And this time, when they veered around it, they saw something. It was a light at the end of the tunnel – literally. In fact, it looked like sunlight!

The tunnel began to slope upwards. The girls were climbing up – and out – of the portal. Cornelia began breathing harder. What on earth would they find at the end of the portal?

What am I thinking, Cornelia asked herself, shaking her head lightly. The question is, what on this *non*-earth will we find? We're not in Heatherfield anymore.

Suddenly, Will stumbled. She slapped one hand onto the wall and used the other to support her head, which suddenly seemed too heavy to hold upright.

"Huh," she muttered woozily. "It's that sensation again. It's really strong this time."

"Of course," Hay Lin said, running up to throw a sympathetic arm around Will's shoulders. "We're in Metamoor now."

Will nodded weakly. Then, as it had before, the dizziness seemed to leave her quickly. She straightened up and squared her shoulders. The girls were only a few yards away from the end of the tunnel. Light was streaming in now, bathing them in a golden glow.

Will rushed towards the exit and hopped out into . . . Metamoor? As Cornelia poked her head out of the portal, she gasped.

This wasn't some strange land at all! It was a place with grass and trees, half-covered in autumn leaves. It was a place in which there were both sunlight and Elyon's purple house – with a gaping hole in the wall.

"O-*kaaaay*," Hay Lin said, looking around in bewilderment. "Maybe we're not in Metamoor after all."

# TWELVE

Will felt her wings fluttering behind her. She glanced over her newly broadened shoulder. The shimmery feathers were trembling and quaking.

It's almost like having a dog's tail! she marveled. My wings are totally broadcasting my mood. And at the moment, they're colouring me confused.

Because Hay Lin was right. This place the portal had brought them to didn't seem Metamoorish at all. Not that Will had had any idea what Metamoor would be like. But she'd pictured a gloomy place, filled with shadows and sinister figures. She'd pictured anything but this. She noted the same overgrown grass they'd left in Elyon's yard an hour before. They'd finished their crazy journey right back where they'd started.

"Gee," Cornelia said dryly. "Guess we took a wrong turn."

"That's so strange," Will blurted out. She took a few halting steps forward. The grass was flattened silently beneath her knee-high purple boots. Will looked up at some leaves dangling from a branch above her head. They were shimmering in a breeze, just getting ready to break free and fall to the ground.

Will squinted at the leaves. Something was strange about them. But what was it?

Suddenly, Will realised what it was.

"Listen," she said to her friends. "No noises!"

She pointed to the leaves. While the other girls looked quizzically at the branch, Will craned her ear for a faint whistle of wind. For the rustling of the dried-out leaves. A bird. A car whooshing through the street. Anything.

But all she heard was silence.

"There's nobody around," she exclaimed, spinning around in a circle. The sidewalks were empty. There wasn't a bus or bicycle or skateboard in sight. The city seemed to be completely and utterly abandoned.

"Look!" Irma said, interrupting Will's survey of this new, strange Heatherfield. "There's someone over there!"

Irma pointed across the street and began to run towards a tall, stucco house. A man was hurrying up its steps to the front door. He was wearing an ordinary, tan trench coat and carrying a leather briefcase. He glanced over his shoulder as Irma called out, "Sir! Please, sir!"

The man jumped and began fumbling in his coat pocket for his house keys. He moved closer to the door and unlocked it quickly.

"Don't run away!" Irma cried. "Wait!"

By now, all five girls were running towards the man. But before they could reach him, the pale-faced grown-up slipped inside the house and slammed the door shut.

"Sir!" Irma cried desperately.

Will sighed. She couldn't *totally* blame the guy for being weirded-out. How often do you see five teenage girls in matching, slinky outfits parading along the streets of Heatherfield? Will glanced over her shoulder at her twittering feathers.

And I almost forgot the weirdest part of all,

she thought, clapping a hand to her forehead. Our wings! We must make for quite a bizarre picture.

But, Irma didn't seem to understand why anyone would be afraid of them, much less refuse to help them. She thumped up the front steps of the house and began pounding on the door.

"Please open up," she called. "I just want to talk to you– "

Irma's words were suddenly swallowed in a gasp.

She stepped backwards.

"N– now that I'm a magical being," she stammered, "I guess I don't know my own strength!"

Will peered past Irma.

A crack had formed in the middle of the door – right where Irma had been banging on it. Like a spiderweb, the fissure began extending out to the corners of the door. Pretty soon, the wood was divided into several pieces.

"What have you done?" Taranee demanded from the bottom of the steps.

"Don't look at me like that!" Irma squealed, turning around to look at the accusing faces of her friends. "It's not my fault!"

*Krrrr-POOOOWWWWW!*

"*Eeeeeeek!*" the girls screamed in unison.

The cracked door had just exploded. Shards of it flew in every direction.

When Will looked up, she realised the devastation wasn't limited to the door! The entire *house* was cracking into jagged pieces. And those pieces were beginning to tumble down upon the girls.

"*Aaaaaigh!*" Will cried. She watched her friends cringe and collapse to the porch floor, covering their heads in terror. They didn't have time to run.

Will threw her own hands over her head and hoped that somehow her magic would protect her from the shower of bricks, roof tiles, glass, and gutters.

*CRA-A-ASH!*

Something had landed a few inches from Will's right ear. She jumped and peeked through her folded arms. She expected to see a chunk of splintered stone or maybe a shattered windowpane lying next to her.

Instead, she saw a flat and mysterious object. It was a triangle of something that looked like very thick cardboard. When Will grabbed it, it felt heavy and gluey in her hands. It was of a putty-grey colour.

"Huh," Will said, sitting up slowly. She turned the triangle over in her hands and gasped. The cardboard was painted with incredibly real-looking bricks.

With wide eyes, Will looked up at the still-careening bits of house.

*All* the pieces were flat and thin! It was *fake*, like a theater set!

The strangeness wasn't limited to that particular house. Gazing down the street, Will saw the entire block collapsing. First, the buildings broke into bits of cardboard litter. Then, after hitting the ground, the buildings evaporated into quickly dissipating clouds of dust.

The entire street – the entire city – was nothing but a facade.

The thing about a facade, Will thought fearfully, is that there's always something behind it.

When the dust from all the falling debris had cleared, Will got shakily to her feet to see just what that something was. Her first glimpse of her surroundings filled her with confusion.

A second glimpse filled her with fear.

It wasn't until the other girls had stood up and clustered around Will in a protective huddle of limbs and wings that Will truly began to comprehend everything she was seeing.

"Gee," Irma whispered. "I think it's pretty clear now. . . . This is *definitely* not our Heatherfield."

Will nodded. She couldn't speak. She was too busy gazing around her.

They were most definitely not in Heatherfield anymore, but they *were* in a city – a city that looked positively medieval. The buildings were tall and narrow, with stone foundations, and were topped with round, wooden battlements. They were supported by creaky ramparts, and their windows were small and dusty.

The girls stood on a muddy, narrow street. Behind them was an austere, stone staircase. It curved around another imposing building – built into a rocky hill – then ducked under a curved aqueduct before snaking up the side of a hill.

Will had seen a movie once that had been set in Shakespeare's time, hundreds of years earlier. It had looked something like this. Except –

"Guys?" Taranee said in a trembling voice. She pointed up at something clinging to one of the stone walls.

Will sucked in her breath quickly.

Okay, she thought in panic, that's *definitely* not Romeo *or* Juliet.

No, it was a creepy creature that resembled an iguana – a bright, blue iguana, splashed with spattery-looking, green markings. Its powder-blue tongue flickered tauntingly. It gazed at the girls quizzically . . . and almost intelligently.

Then Will noticed something else that was odd about the curly-tailed beast. It was wearing clothes! A frayed, brown tunic with a leather belt, to be exact.

*Skitter-skitter-skitter.*

Will jumped and grabbed Taranee's arm.

"What was that?" she whispered. Out of the corner of her eye, Will saw Hay Lin gaping at a ten-foot-long, orange-and-green tail slithering lazily through the street. It was undulating around a corner. The tail's enormous owner was clearly halfway down the block already.

Will had only to glance up to get an eyeful of more grotesque creatures: a crouching, dragonlike critter wearing a green vest, and figures that walked upright on two legs but definitely did *not* resemble people (it was the pointy ears and ice-blue skin that clued Will in). There were squat creatures and scaly creatures and–

"Hello, Guardians!"

A welcoming committee! Will thought with a shudder.

Together, the five girls spun around. They found themselves gazing down a wide street. It was a dark, dreary stretch of mud made claustrophobic by the half-crumbling buildings looming over it.

"*Uh-oh,*" Will whispered.

She heard the mysterious, threatening voice again.

"We've been waiting for you for a long time," it said. The voice was gravelly and smooth, all at the same time. The voice was also . . . familiar.

Finally, the owner of the voice showed his face – complete with slithering tail, scaly, green skin, razorlike jaw, and jaggedy teeth. His malevolent eyes were cloaked behind a pulsing red mask.

With this scaly beast appeared the giant

blue thug who'd tried to harm the Guardians several times already. Together, the two stepped through the throng of soldiers to confront the girls head on. The beast was dressed in some sort of robe – a dramatic swath of blue fabric, emblazoned with the Seal of Phobos.

Will's limbs started to tremble. But then she clenched her fists and ordered herself not to lose it. She had to be strong! She had to concentrate on whatever the snaky creature had to say.

"As you see," he announced. "I didn't come alone."

Will thought he was referring to his army of thugs. But then, a figure stepped out from behind the villain. That figure was also draped in blue robes with the Seal of Phobos on them. But the blue-draped presence wasn't some grotesque, otherworldly creature. It was Elyon!

"Say hello to your friends, Elyon," the beast said, looming over the small girl with a creepy smile.

Will – with her friends at her heels – ran up to Elyon and grabbed her hands. Will's magical self was several inches taller than Elyon. She leaned down and looked into Elyon's pale eyes. They were vibrant, even laughing. The somber ghost the girls had encountered in the basement was nowhere to be seen.

"Elyon!" Will gasped. "What have they done to you?"

"Nothing! I'm fine!" Elyon said with a grin. "I'm happy to see you!"

Will shook her head in confusion and grasped Elyon's hands more tightly.

"We're going home, and you're coming with us!" she blurted out. "You can't stay here in this horrible place."

Elyon laughed.

"Ah," she said, pulling her hands from Will's and waving her friend away jovially. "You don't understand. This horrible place has a name, you know. Welcome, my friends, to Meridian, the city at the heart of Metamoor. Welcome to my home!"

Elyon looked each one of them in the eye with a warm smile.

"Stay," she said, enticingly. "You'll like it!"

Irma crossed her arms and looked askance at the dank-looking buildings that surrounded them.

"Sure," she said, with sarcasm. "I may ask my parents to rent a house here for the summer."

Seemingly stung by Irma's rejection, Elyon took a step backward, to stand in the shelter of the scaly beast's vast cloak. He loomed above her, framing her in evil.

Elyon's face had darkened as well. Her eyes grew heavy-lidded and her mouth twisted into an ugly sneer.

"You don't want to stay?" she asked softly. "I'm so sorry."

"You leave us with no choice," the snakeman added. Then he glanced over his shoulder at the horde of armed creatures.

"Guards!" he barked. "Take them!"

Hay Lin grabbed Will by the arm.

"I knew he was going to say that!" she wailed. "I knew it!"

Will reached out and pushed her four friends from behind her. Then she raised her own arms in front of her face. Her hands were already shooting forth pink sparks.

"Don't let them get any closer!" Will ordered her fellow Guardians.

And from that moment on, the five girls

began to work as one. It didn't matter that their first practise session had ended in a mud bath. Or that Taranee feared her magic. Or that Cornelia resented hers.

Because, now, the Heart of Candracar – and their friendship – was pulling them all together. And together, they would fight off this army of thugs.

A blast of pink magic shot from Will's palms. It hit a cluster of soldiers right at their feet, unbalancing them and sending them flying onto their backs.

Meanwhile, Hay Lin hurled a blast of air at another charging soldier. It caught him in the gut. He went soaring! The soldier screamed and flailed until he hit a stone building with a sickening thud. He fell to the muddy street and lay still.

Behind Will, a soldier was bearing down on Taranee. Will was sure her friend must be quaking. She started to run to her aid.

But then she skidded to a halt.

"Taranee?" she murmured.

There was nothing fearful about Taranee now. In fact, she was downright bold! She thrust one hand toward the soldier as he rushed toward her. Her palm glowed orange as she began to rev up for magic.

"Hey," Taranee admonished the thug. "Never hit a woman, especially with a red-hot sword!"

With that, she threw a fiery stream of magic. It hit the soldier's sword with a shower of sparks. Immediately, the weapon took on a neon-orange glow. It turned sizzling and molten. The soldier dropped his sword.

Will grinned. Then she spun around to face more soldiers.

We're doing it, she thought incredulously. We're really doing it. We're fighting them off with our magic!

We are powerful.

We are magical.

We are a united force.

We are Guardians of the Veil!

Will hurled another blast at an attacking soldier and watched with grim satisfaction as her power sent him flying.

Her exultation didn't last long, though. The Guardians were winning – she could see that. But that didn't mean this battle was going to be easy. Or quick.

This is just the beginning, Will thought as she gave her friends a grateful glance. We've got a long, hard fight ahead of us. But together, I think we're gonna make it!

STAY! YOU'LL LIKE IT!

SURE! I'LL ASK MY PARENTS TO RENT A HOUSE HERE FOR THE SUMMER!

YOU DON'T WANT TO STAY? I'M SO SORRY.

YOU LEAVE US WITH NO CHOICE. . . .

GUARDS! SEIZE THEM!

I KNEW HE WAS GOING TO SAY THAT! I KNEW IT!

BZZL BZZAP

DON'T LET THEM GET ANY CLOSER!

WOOOOSHH

RAAAAARGH!

POW!

HEY! NEVER HIT A WOMAN. . . .

. . . ESPECIALLY WITH A RED-HOT SWORD!

FSSS

YEOW!